"Maybe I'm confused," said Felicia. *"**What** is a cowboy?"*

Jackson lifted his chin, narrowed his eyes. "Being a cowboy means having a code. A nobility that went out of style." He paused. "A cowboy can stand and face anything that shows up to beat him down."

Felicia wanted to touch him again, to make sure he was real, to make sure she wasn't conjuring a guy who thought in simple poetry and believed in old-fashioned values.

Jack waved his commentary away. "Show me someone like that, and you'll see a real cowboy."

She wished she could tell him her definition, too: a man who had the power to give her everything she'd always yearned for. As they parked in front of the store, she couldn't help asking one more question.

"So there's no hope left for the myth, the cowboy?"

Jack stared straight ahead, a smile on his lips. "Maybe there's one left."

Dear Reader,

This beautiful month of April we have six very special reads for you, starting with *Falling for the Boss* by Elizabeth Harbison, this month's installment in our FAMILY BUSINESS continuity. Watch what happens when two star-crossed high school sweethearts get a second chance—only this time they're on opposite sides of the boardroom table! Next, bestselling author RaeAnne Thayne pays us a wonderful and emotional visit in Special Edition with her new miniseries, THE COWBOYS OF COLD CREEK. In *Light the Stars,* the first book in the series, a frazzled single father is shocked to hear that his mother (not to mention babysitter) eloped—with a supposed scam artist. So what is he to do when said scam artist's lovely daughter turns up on his doorstep? Find out (and don't miss next month's book in this series, *Dancing in the Moonlight*). In Patricia McLinn's *What Are Friends For?,* the first in her SEASONS IN A SMALL TOWN duet, a female police officer is reunited—with the guy who got away. Maybe she'll be able to detain him this time….

Jessica Bird concludes her MOOREHOUSE LEGACY series with *From the First,* in which Alex Moorehouse finally might get the woman he could never stop wanting. Only problem is, she's a recent widow—and her late husband was Alex's best friend. In Karen Sandler's *Her Baby's Hero,* a couple looks for that happy ending even though the second time they meet, she's six months' pregnant with his twins! And in *The Last Cowboy* by Crystal Green, a woman desperate for motherhood learns that "the last cowboy will make you a mother." But real cowboys don't exist anymore…or do they?

So enjoy, and don't forget to come back next month. Everything will be in bloom….

Have fun.

Gail Chasan
Senior Editor

Please address questions and book requests to:
Silhouette Reader Service
U.S.: 3010 Walden Ave., P.O. Box 1325, Buffalo, NY 14269
Canadian: P.O. Box 609, Fort Erie, Ont. L2A 5X3

THE LAST
COWBOY

CRYSTAL GREEN

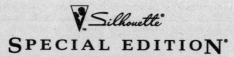

Published by Silhouette Books

America's Publisher of Contemporary Romance

To Rich, Stefania and Jason, my wonderful league of
friends. Thank you for your support and all the fun.

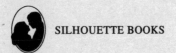 SILHOUETTE BOOKS

ISBN 0-373-24752-4

THE LAST COWBOY

Copyright © 2006 by Chris Marie Green

Visit Silhouette Books at www.eHarlequin.com

Printed in U.S.A.

CRYSTAL GREEN

Crystal Green lives near Las Vegas, Nevada, where she writes for Silhouette Special Edition and Bombshell, plus Harlequin Blaze. She loves to read, overanalyze movies, do yoga and write about her travels and obsessions on her Web site, www.crystal-green.com. There, you can read about her trips on Route 66 as well as visits to Japan and Italy.

She'd love to hear from her readers by e-mail through the "Contact Crystal" feature on her Web page!

EMMY'S APPLE CRISP

6 cups sliced, pared apples
2 tbsp orange juice
⅔ cup brown sugar, packed
⅓ cup unsifted flour
½ tsp grated orange rind
⅓ cup butter or regular margarine
sweetened whipped cream

Arrange apples in 8-inch square baking pan.
Sprinkle apples with orange juice. Combine brown
sugar, flour and orange rind in a bowl. Cut in butter
with pastry blender or two forks until mixture is
crumbly. Sprinkle crumb mixture over apples. Bake
in 375°F oven 40 minutes or until apples are tender.
Place on rack and cool slightly. Spoon crisp into
dessert dishes. Top with sweetened whipped cream.

Makes 6 helpings.

Serve with lots of love.

Chapter One

After walking this earth for forty-two years, Jackson North had drifted through enough fights to know how to deal with a sticky situation.

If you were in a bar and a roughneck didn't take too kindly to the way you sipped a beer, buy him enough to either make him your buddy or make him pass out. If you felt a pair of eyes boring into you from across a smoke-shrouded room, never look up from the table to acknowledge the threat. And if worst ever came to worst, let the fists fly and worry about the damage later.

But Jackson was exhausted these days. Too bone-weary to play peacemaker, too disillusioned to care about much of anything anymore.

That's why—when he felt the punch skim past him only to miss the victim standing on the other side of his body—Jackson actually thought of turning tail and running from this particular confrontation.

He tensed and glanced down at the battling little boy and girl.

The punch thrower came perilously close to leaning against Jackson while taunting his opponent.

"I'm gonna get you, Alina!"

"Nah-nah-nah-nah-nah!" said the girl tot who was hovering ever closer to Jackson's other leg.

They were closing in. It was harder to breathe now.

Why'd this have to go and happen? Here he'd been, perfectly content to linger on the fringes of the party when the two children had burst out of nowhere. They'd caught Jackson off guard when they'd sprinted over to him from the main lawn of Oakvale Ranch—where pony rides, a chili cook-off, games and carnival attractions were sending off sparks of laughter and country-western music.

Damn Rip McCain for dragging Jackson and the ranch's few other workers over here, all but forcing them to be social and "mingle with the neighbor people." Hell. It was bad enough that Jackson's most recent home—the Hanging R—would soon see the arrival of Old Rip's great-nephew, who'd recently lost his parents and didn't have any other relatives to take him in.

Dammit, if Jackson had known there'd be a little boy living with them, he wouldn't have hired on just over a month ago. If—

The sound of a razzing tongue distracted him.

"Stop that, Konrad," the young girl said from Jackson's right flank. "I'm telling Mom on you."

This time, the razzer did lean into Jackson's leg. The touch completely froze him, lodging his heart in his throat. Memories of two other children—his sons—threatened to crush him.

"Kids…" The word choked out of him as he helplessly raised his hands out of their way.

He should've retreated from the discomfort that was slowly enveloping him, but when he'd first gotten to this Leukemia Society fund-raiser, he'd made the unfortunate choice of standing with his back to one of the festive tents, cutting himself off from all human contact.

Cutting himself off from an escape, too.

As Alina swatted at Konrad, the boy hugged Jackson's leg. Jackson's three-year-old son, Lucas, used to do that—hug his leg.

Back when Jackson had been another man.

Without thinking, he rested his fingertips on this child's head, bringing Konrad to a slow-motion halt as Jackson envisioned Lucas's reddish-brown hair—hair just like his ex-wife's.

As a long-suffering numbness swallowed the wrangler, he remembered five-year-old Leroy's freckled smile, too.

When Konrad glanced up at Jackson, the man jerked his hand away at the toothless surprise of a gaping mouth, an unfamiliar face.

"Konrad! Alina!" said a female voice.

Stepping forward, away from the suddenly quiet children, Jackson nearly bumped into the caller. Instinctively, he reached out, grasping her soft shoulders, steadying her.

Beautiful blue.

Her eyes were all he saw before he averted his gaze, lowering his hands so he could erase the burn of contact by easing his palms against his hips and gripping the denim for some mental balance.

She laughed, but he didn't look back up at her.

"So," she said. "You're all that was keeping the terror twins from ripping each other apart?"

Jackson sort of grunted, hoping that would do for an answer. In the meantime, he tried to distance himself inch by inch, wondering if he could fade into the background again. Wondering if he could get his pulse back to its regular road-to-nowhere speed.

"Well, you two." He could hear her moving toward the twins. "I think you need to say sorry to this man for putting him in the middle of your silliness."

He chanced a wary look while she gathered the kids.

Something in his chest clenched at the sight of her: A light-blue short-sleeved blouse and a wispy ankle-length flowered skirt with a wide-brimmed hat to protect her fair skin against the August sun. Long hair, as white-yellow as the meringue on top of those pies they were selling in one of the charity food tents. And when she tilted her head toward him and smiled, he got a second gander at those eyes: as playful as a kitten's, tipped up at the corners, a twinkling shade of blue.

She was almost a throwback to simpler times. A prairie girl full of light and innocence, caught in a museum painting or a fantasy of days gone by.

Jackson cleared his throat and squinted. He'd been gaping. Might as well face the music.

"If the kids here apologize to anyone," he said, "it should probably be to each other. Not to me."

The little boy shrugged. "We fight all the time."

"Yeah," the girl agreed.

Growling in mock frustration, the blonde pretended to grab the twins' ears. "You're both a real big help to your mom. Here she is, just out of the hospital with another baby, and you're running around wreaking havoc. Why, I oughta…"

She made an ear-twisting motion with her hands and the twins giggled.

Jackson took a couple more steps back, chest heavy with things he'd rather forget. Family. Kids. Inevitable anguish.

"We'll be good, Felicia," the girl said, hugging the blonde.

Not to be outdone, the boy joined the embrace. "Don't be mad at us."

She laughed again, her words muffled by their enthusiastic cradling. "I *will* be mad if I see you going after each other again. I'm serious."

Unable to help it, Jackson found his eyes glued to her once more.

"Go to your mom." She hustled the twins away, pointing toward a well-padded woman holding a swaddled infant and standing near a tiny merry-go-round. The kids took off, greeting their mother with clumsy energy.

The blonde didn't move for a moment, just kept her gaze on them. A sad sort of gaze. The corners of her mouth twitched once before she sighed and crossed her arms over her chest.

The sounds of carnival music mixed with a Clint Black song, filling the silence between them. Finally, she straightened up and walked toward him, all cheer and sunshine once again.

"I really am sorry about that."

"Forget it." Could he leave without Rip getting all over his case for being a curmudgeon?

Then again, did he really want to go now that the day had become a little more interesting?

She was close enough so he could smell her perfume—something as pure as summer petals.

Closing his eyes, Jackson tried to fight whatever it was that addled his brain. He was beyond flirtation and intimacy. Had been for years.

When he looked again, she was sticking out her hand. "I'm Felicia Markowski. I work in housekeeping here at Oakvale. And those were two of many, many second cousins."

He hesitated to accept her touch, entertained a slew of curse words in his mind then slid his fingers into her gentle grip. Still, Jackson didn't allow himself the luxury of enjoying her skin. Instead, he ignored the warmth, the tingling bolt of awareness that jagged through his body.

He disconnected.

"Jackson North," he said. "Hanging R."

"Really?" She didn't seem to mind that he'd just about treated her handshake like a man whipping off a clinging snake that'd buried its fangs into him. "Old Rip hasn't hired anyone in ages."

Discomfited, Jackson hoped he could leave soon.

"I'm surprised he took on another employee," she added, "what with all the rumors about the ranch being in such bad shape. We all love Rip McCain to death, but he wouldn't ask for help even if it started licking his ankles and begging for attention."

Jackson thought of the Hanging R's dilapidated buildings, the dwindling stock of longhorn cattle, the rusted tools and broken fences.

But he didn't say squat.

She must've noticed him fidgeting like a teenage boy who'd been caught climbing out of a girl's window with his pants around his ankles. Her smile was way too amused to be casual.

"So you go by Jackson, huh? If we're going to be neighbors, can I call you Jack?"

She wouldn't be calling him anything once he finally got back to the ranch and stayed there. "If it pulls your trigger. Sure."

"It does." A laugh bubbled out of her. "What brings you to these parts, *Jack?*"

"I… Well, what brings most wranglers to a ranch?"

"Oh, a private man. Got it." She didn't seem very put off by his clammed-up-ness. In fact, she was being so warm and welcoming that he could've mistaken it for something deeper.

Attraction?

Sure. Gorgeous blondes were *always* drawn to men like him: as craggy as the face of a mountain, old enough to be her babysitter. And plenty of off-putting attitude to boot.

Might as well leave while the leaving was good—before he found himself in an actual conversation. He hated those. Hated having to make excuses when it came time to take the next step with a woman.

Damned divorce, he thought. Damned fear.

Tipping his hat in farewell, he started to walk off, to be alone again.

Just then, a gust of wind stirred the air and the woman's own straw hat huffed off her head.

Had it been his imagination, or had she let it go a little too easily?

"Oops," she said, sounding much too innocuous.

As the hat rolled over the neatly manicured lawn, he stepped over, scooped it up and returned it.

"Thank you." She positively beamed at him, as if he'd gathered her into his arms to carry her over a muddy puddle or had plucked her puppy dog from a flood.

Would it be a bad thing to preen a little under her appreciation? He did—until he forced himself to stop. "It was nothing."

Unable to help it, he found himself peering at her again. Caught her giving him the once-over, too, her gaze slowly traveling up his body from boot to hat.

A flare of pure lust consumed him, unwelcome in its heat, its unguarded possibilities. He cleared his throat.

She blushed, smiled again, then started walking

at a speed that invited him to keep pace. Like some kind of wood puppet, he did.

There'd been a time when he'd have followed a beautiful woman anywhere. Maybe feeling unhindered again—even for just a few minutes—wouldn't do any harm.

Right?

Besides, maybe he could tolerate being neighborly until he made it to the exit.

As they strolled, matching steps, he said to himself, *This is nice. Right nice, actually.*

Nearing the quaint midway, they passed the twins and their mother, and all of them waved. The woman held a hand over one of her baby's ears and called, "Polka, Felicia! An hour and a half! You'll be there?"

Felicia gave a thumbs-up and when she turned back to him, there was a certain sorrow taking the place of the twinkle in her eyes, though he could tell she was doing her best to hide it.

"She's another cousin—a first, this time. And the baby's named Stan, another second cousin." There was a catch in her voice. But maybe he'd imagined it, because in the next instant, she was back to flashing a smile at him. "How about I introduce you to another neighbor or two?"

"I've…got to get back. Work. You know." Why the hell did he sound so stiff, so uncomfortable? It was almost as if he'd never met a female before. Had he withdrawn from normal life so much these last few years that he couldn't socialize properly now?

"I could walk you out then," she said.

Tempted but…no. First it'd be a walk to the gate. Then an invitation to dinner. Then commitment. Then children….

He couldn't breathe again.

Shaking his head, he pointed toward the exit. "Not necessary. Thanks for the offer."

She laughed. "You're not much for chatting, are you?" There was still a teasing lightness to her, making Jackson too aware that her youth and exuberance created a canyon of years between them, even if they had been walking side by side.

Dammit, he was the world's biggest crab, wasn't he? Couldn't he relax, even a little?

This woman kind of made him want to try.

He jerked his head at the merry-go-round, back at the twins and their mother. "Your cousin, huh?"

Hell, it wasn't brilliant conversation, but definitely a start.

"If you look around, you'll see my entire clan running amuck." She gestured toward a crowd of squealing brunette children by the ring toss who were pounding each other with the stuffed animals they must have won.

"You're all from around these parts?"

There, he was getting better at this by the second.

"You bet. We come from generations of good Polish stock who settled here over a hundred years ago. If you've been to town, you've probably seen the church. My relatives helped build it during the last half of the nineteenth century."

He nodded, even though, so far, he'd visited Wycliffe's bars more often than any church.

They reached the heart of the midway, surrounded by the music stage, more rides and charity booths. The aroma of fried foods and cotton candy laced the air. In front of them, a table decorated with a crystal ball and sheer red material waited. A sign reading Back in a Flash was taped to a chair.

As they stood there, Jackson noticed that they were drawing stares and hopeful glances from most of the folks in the area.

Now he was feeling strange again, especially since they all seemed to have some kind of expectation in the lift of their brows.

"Don't mind them," Felicia said. "Everyone's a matchmaker around here. But all you have to do is make small talk with every single girl you meet today, and the pressure will be off. You'll get a flighty reputation no *ehevermittler* will want to touch."

He probably looked confused at the foreign word, as well as her reasoning.

"*Ehevermittler.* German for matchmaker, the

curse of my existence." She shrugged, the gesture pretty adorable. "Yeah, German—my mom's side. The hundreds of cousins you see are melting pots, too, just like me. Pop's side of the family is where I get my polka skills, and…"

She cut herself off. "I'm talking a lot, aren't I?"

He opened his mouth to answer. Sure, she was sort of like a windmill in a gale, but he wasn't minding so much now. He'd probably never even see her again after today, so why worry?

"It's an issue I'm trying to overcome," she said, "talking a lot. I'm trying to make you feel at home, and I'm overcompensating, I think."

She took another breath to continue, then stopped, gaze fixed on a passing cluster of elderly women who were staring at Felicia with what seemed like pity. As she glanced away, they did, too, shaking their heads.

What had that been about?

"Well," Felicia said, ignoring her neighbors and gesturing toward the table, "this is my last stop. I'm helping to collect money for the Society here."

Jackson motioned toward the crystal ball. "The fortune-teller's booth?"

"You've got it. Do you want Madame Carlota to divine your future? Riches, happiness…romance?"

Stepping away from the table, Jackson made his answer abundantly clear. If tomorrow was anything like his yesterdays, he didn't want to know.

Felicia must have read his body language because, even though she kept up the peppy smile, her shoulders dropped, almost as if he'd let her down somehow.

Was she one of those women who pounced on every new man who moved into the area? If so, he was better off making his desire to be left alone even more obvious.

"I'll leave you to your crystal gazing," he said, tipping his hat at her again, then digging into his wallet for a twenty-dollar bill and handing it to her. "Put this in the pot."

"Sure you don't want your money's worth?"

Tightness closed his throat and, as he lifted his hand in goodbye, he also turned to go. But, in his rush to get back to normalcy, he brushed against another woman.

She was a svelte brunette with light-brown skin, a flowing fortune-teller's costume and straight dark hair covered with a gypsy scarf. Her deep brown sloe eyes blinked up at him as he passed her, his knuckles accidentally skimming her bared arm.

In that moment, Jackson felt like a book that was being read.

He apologized, then did what self-preservation dictated: he blocked her out and headed back to the safety of his own four walls.

A place where no one could look past his frown and discover what lay beneath.

Chapter Two

Through a haze of fascination, Felicia watched Jack North amble out of the crowd then disappear.

Wow.

It wasn't that he was handsome. Not in a traditional sense, with those squinting dark eyes that were caged by emerging wrinkles and heavy brows. Eyes that were unfathomable and magnetic, drawing her into their depths. Underneath his hat, she'd even caught a glimpse of silver in his black hair.

What was so appealing about him then?

Felicia was normally drawn to men who were younger, more accessible, their skin unlined instead of rough-hewn, their smiles ready and eager instead of nonexistent.

Jackson North wasn't normal crush material. He was a cowpoke carved into an uneven length of pine, sturdy and lean, stoic and hard edged.

So why was her body singing? Okay, maybe it was just humming—and she really shouldn't be getting carried away with a guy so fast again—but…

Carlota Verde came to stand next to her, yet Felicia barely registered her best friend and fellow maid because she was so deep in this dopey instant attraction.

"Wow," Felicia whispered.

"Tell me about it."

Slowly, Carlota assumed solid form in Felicia's sights. She had one hand propped on her skirted hip and one palm against her scarf-covered head, almost as if she'd gotten one of her horrible headaches.

This was how Carlota's premonitions always came—via migraine. Felicia and their good friend Emmy had lived with Carlota's touch of magic all their lives. The random psychic vibes were just a part of her personality, as unremarkable as her taste for Chet Baker's music or her driven, yet ultimately doomed, need to play the guitar.

She'd decided to lend her visionary talents to today's charity event after a little persuasion from their boss, Mrs. Rhodes. Even if Carlota's predictions couldn't be summoned with the regularity of clockwork, she still had a quick mind and the wit of an entertainer. The Leukemia Society patrons would love her, Mrs. Rhodes had said, even if she were slinging bull instead of always dishing out the real thing.

But now, as Carlota shook off whatever was bothering her, Felicia touched her friend's shoulder, concerned.

"You okay?"

"*Sí,* no problem. Just a twinge of something." Carlota took a big breath, then grinned, sticking a thumb toward the departed Jack. "Are you drooling over…?"

"Drooling?" Felicia tried the clueless act. "Me?"

"You've got that crazy smile and stars in your eyes. Again."

"Right. Again." Crush number 1,036. She was excellent at cultivating schoolgirl dreams, but when it came to hanging on to a man…

"He's much too old for you," Carlota said. "Maybe not in years, but in mileage. I felt his energy. He's dark inside, like an empty room with the lights turned off."

"Are you warning me away from him, Madame Carlota?"

"Of course not. I can't tell a stubborn twenty-five-year-old woman who's supposedly reached maturity what to do." And with that, the sassy maid nudged Felicia in amusement, took her break sign down, sat in her chair and opened for business, putting an end to the conversation.

Right away, patrons lined up to hear their fortunes, and Felicia busied herself by collecting money and chatting with the waiting crowd. Several of them had obviously seen her with Jack North, and they were a tad too zealous in questioning her about the newest Hanging R employee.

Dear old busybodies.

Everyone knew about Felicia's business and she knew about theirs in return. Wycliffe was a tight-knit community, and her relatives and neighbors were always offering advice.

And they *all* knew about Felicia's deepest pain, even if she did her darnedest to avoid it.

Even now, women strolled down the modest midway, their arms linked with husbands while their sons and daughters followed in their parents' tracks. Watching them, Felicia once again felt so alone, circled by women with their children and the men who wanted wives who could have those children.

Her heart wrenched, almost as if it were bending backward to look away.

When someone's arm wrapped around Felicia's shoulders, she cheered up, telling herself that mulling over her problems wouldn't do any good.

It was Emmy, one of the best friends Felicia had ever known. She, Carlota and Felicia had been raised together here at Oakvale, the daughters of servants who'd worked for the Rhodes family generation after generation. They'd banded together, three of a kind, supporting each other through broken dreams and the changes brought on by passing years.

Now, here stood petite Emmy, holding Felicia with the utmost care, just the same as always. Even though she'd been married for almost a year and had recently given birth to her first child, she was still a newlywed at heart, glowing while wearing her white chef's suit.

Heck, she'd definitely earned the right to glow, Felicia thought, bending to hug Emmy right back.

In the process of falling in love with her husband, Emmy had launched quite the scandal here at Oakvale, catching the eye of *the* Deston Rhodes—yes, the millionaire son of Texas royalty who had been raised on this estate—after he'd mistaken Emmy for another woman. She'd been Oakvale's cook-in-training, and he'd been the resident prince who'd found his Cinderella. Even though Emmy had dug herself a deep hole with her accidental masquerade, their romance had resulted in a happy marriage after all.

Emmy held Felicia at arm's length, assessing her as Carlota finished pretending to tell the fortune of the last customer in line.

"No need to frown, Charlie Brown," Emmy said, smiling with those slightly crooked teeth. "What's going on?"

Felicia squeezed Emmy to her one last time, catching the comforting scent of wood smoke and spices in her friend's short auburn hair. "Done with the chili cook-off?"

"Yup. It'll be the best stuff in the county, no doubt about it." Emmy slid Felicia a sidelong glance. "I thought I'd see if you two needed help while the judges do their thing, but I guess there's something else that needs looking after here."

"We're all out of customers for now," Carlota said, motioning to the empty chairs in front of the table. "Take a load off and listen to Felicia's love song, why don't you?"

"Ah," Emmy said, suddenly understanding why Felicia seemed so glum.

Lovely. As if Felicia wanted to go through this exhausting ritual: meeting a man, sharing it with her friends, getting her hopes up, then standing helplessly by while he got serious ideas about her. She just didn't have the energy for this anymore, especially since that last devastating breakup two months ago.

Toby, there's something I need to tell you....

Her voice echoed in her memory. The out-of-town cowboy had taken her to a posh restaurant, pulling out all the stops in his efforts to tell her that he wanted to bring their relationship to the next level. Sex. Commitment to a future.

By the end of dinner, he'd left her, obviously disappointed by what she'd confessed to him: her shortcomings, the physical imperfections that made having a family a near impossibility for the man she would marry.

Felicia had never been able to voice the details of Toby's breakup to her friends. Maybe it was because part of her felt like giving up from here on out. Maybe it was because telling Emmy and Carlota would bring it all back too painfully.

At any rate, as they sat in front of Carlota, Felicia couldn't work up the bravery to talk about Jack North or her ever-rekindled hopes for a man who would love her no matter what she was lacking.

Even if there was a tiny spark inside her growing with every vivid recollection of him.

"Well," Carlota said to Felicia, her eyes shining with I-hope-this-man-works-for-you verve, "tell Emmy all about him."

"It's no biggie," Felicia said. But even as she uttered it, she smiled, thinking of the way Jack had tipped his hat to her like a gentleman. Thinking of his work-callused hands and how he kept them still and quiet—a man of few words and gestures.

She still didn't understand the attraction, but at

this moment, she would've sworn that he was the most handsome, intriguing male in God's creation.

"All right." Carlota sent a firm nod to Emmy. "*I'll* tell you everything."

Felicia stopped her friend before Carlota could comment on Jack's standoffishness again.

"Okay, okay." She held back a grin. "He's…real interesting."

"Aha." Emmy was clearly bursting at the seams with the need to know more. "Who is he?"

Felicia felt a flush warm her face. "Jackson North."

No one said anything for a moment, maybe because of the way his name still lingered in the air, just like the crackling aftermath of white lightning.

"Jackson North," Carlota repeated. There was a speculative gleam in her gaze. As usual.

Before Felicia knew it, her friend had grabbed her hand, closed her eyes.

"Oh, powers that be," Carlota said in a mock-serious tone, channeling the carnival gypsy—the one who was only here to entertain for charity.

"Carlota, cut it out." Felicia couldn't help laughing. Emmy, too.

The faux fortune-teller continued. "Give me a sign of this woman's future. Show me if Old Rip's new wrangler is Felicia's destiny."

In spite of herself, Felicia held her breath, praying. Though Carlota had received only a few visions about Felicia before—the death of a favorite aunt when she was ten came to mind—she had mainly divined the futures of other people. Near strangers. Random flashes of enlightenment.

Ironic, really, that Felicia and Emmy had rarely been the focus of Carlota's powers. In fact, one of the few times Carlota had predicted anything about Emmy, it had been about Deston and how he was going to pursue their friend until he won her over.

But Felicia had never gotten advance word about her own happily-ever-afters. Maybe because there hadn't been any.

"What do you see, Great One?" Emmy said, playing along.

Dramatically, Carlota opened her eyes. "There will be wonderful love for our Felicia. It'll just take the right man to see past everything that troubles her."

Exactly. Felicia finally exhaled. See, she was back to square one. Unlucky in love but wealthy in friendship.

Not a bad place to be.

Desperate to change the subject, Felicia quickly asked Emmy for a daily update on Nigel, her newborn son. Without pause, Emmy started to gush about her baby and how Deston was even now conducting playtime with Grandma and Grandpa over at "the big house"—Oakvale's regal mansion where Felicia and Carlota still worked as maids. Deston and Emmy had made it a point to bring Nigel over a couple of times per week since Mr. Rhodes—a Texas-sized man with Lone Star–huge appetites—had suffered a minor stroke a couple of months ago. Deston had been devastated, believing that time was their enemy and that he needed to make amends with his domineering father before it was too late.

Felicia listened, enraptured. She loved Nigel like her own and enjoyed hearing every detail about him, especially when the stories pertained to how the powerful, formerly ruthless Mr. Rhodes had been reduced to a baby-talking fool with the child.

Somewhere along the line, they noticed that Carlota was oddly silent.

They turned to their friend, recognizing the closed eyes, the furrowed brow.

A migraine or…?

Felicia got up. "Aspirin."

"No." Carlota rubbed her temple, her golden bracelets clanking like eerie music. "That was no normal headache."

Emmy pulled a cautious Felicia back down to her seat.

"Weird," Carlota said. "Usually I *see* what's happening after I touch someone, right? But this time, there was just fire. Heat. Words." Perplexed, she looked at Felicia. "'The last cowboy's going to make you a mother.'"

Felicia's stomach fluttered as she leaned forward. Questions scratched at her throat.

No, Carlota had to be wrong. The doctors had already told her she might not be able to have a baby. Not with her endometriosis. In fact, odds were so abysmally low that everyone knew Felicia as "the unlucky Markowski"—a label she tried her best to live with.

"The last cowboy," Carlota whispered. "A mother, Felicia. *A mother.*"

Hope started to race around Felicia's veins. She didn't want to start chasing it. It'd just break her heart in the end.

Emmy's eyes were wide and excited. "Are you sure, Carlota?"

Their friend nodded, but Emmy needn't have asked anyway. Carlota took power from touch, reading the skin. Even though she didn't always get a vibe—especially from her friends—she was careful about physical contact. It put a real damper on her own personal life because, more often than not, the act of touching told her more than she wanted to know about a person.

Emmy bit her lip and caught Felicia's gaze, her eyes tearing up. As for Felicia, she could barely even move.

Gulping, Emmy squeezed Felicia's arm. She was probably thinking the same thing. *A mom? How?*

Maybe Carlota was wrong this time. She very rarely was, but still…

Felicia's heart wouldn't stop pumping, building, priming itself for another crash she would only pretend to recover from.

"I'm not sure how this is going to happen," she said, trying to stay sunny even though doubts were pulling her down. "We all know I won't be having babies."

No one said anything for a moment. Felicia's endometriosis—which could cause infertility—was something she'd lived with for about two years now, ever since it'd been diagnosed. In her own mind, the stigma defined her, even if her neighbors and friends never talked about it to outsiders—especially the men she often met at rodeos, men outside the community. Yup, Wycliffe made sure she had a chance to find a good man who wouldn't be biased against her shortcomings, bless them.

But that didn't change how the doctors had told her she'd probably developed the condition, where scar tissue ultimately formed on her reproductive organs and disabled them, when she was a teen. She should've known, with all those painful periods, the tenderness in her right ovary during her first exam.

But that hadn't been the worst of it. Her "problem" had become especially painful in light of her wildly breeding family and the way they tried to sneak those sympathetic glances past Felicia when they thought she wasn't looking.

"Maybe surgery will work for you after all," Emmy said, "no matter what the doctors say."

Felicia was scheduled for laser treatment in a few months, for better or worse. Heck, she had to try, even if the odds weren't good. Even if the doctors said her symptoms would probably reoccur afterward—if the experts were even successful in healing her in the first place.

Brushing away the thread of emptiness winding through her, Felicia said, "More than one doctor has told me it probably won't help my birthing gear. They should know."

Her friends looked so crushed for her.

"I'll adopt someday," she continued, brightening, repeating her mantra.

And she didn't mind the thought of it. Really. She could love someone else's natural child just as much as her own.

Emmy reached for her hand, laid her own over it. "But what Carlota said—"

"—I'm always right." Their friend tightened her jaw.

Maybe not, this time, Felicia thought. After all, how could Carlota know more than doctors?

"Where's the girl who believes in angels?" Emmy

asked, squeezing Felicia's fingers, transferring some hope through her friend's skin.

She was right. Where was that girl? Was she with the last piece of her broken heart on that trail of crumbled relationships she'd left behind?

Carlota had fisted her own hands, confident in her abilities to the end. "All we need to do is find out who this last cowboy is. Then everything will fall into place."

They wanted to believe this prediction as much as she did. God, this was cruel, to hang hope in front of her like a carrot she'd be chasing for the rest of her life.

But, at the same time, she knew Carlota wouldn't joke about this.

She was dead serious.

"I've got it," Emmy said, brown eyes alight. "Toby. Toby Baker is the *last cowboy* Felicia dated. What if…?"

No, Felicia thought. Not Toby.

They didn't know about the disgust on his face when Felicia had told him about her condition.

"He's not my biological savior, you all. Carlota's got her wires crossed."

"Last cowboy," Carlota mumbled, determined to solve this, hardly even part of the conversation anymore.

Inside, Felicia started to quiver, her body so tired

of wishing, of holding in all the dreams. Of feeling incomplete.

Last cowboy.

Mother.

Could it really happen? All her life, she'd tried to "do unto others," to be an optimist. Was this fate's way of ending the games and rewarding her patience?

Of giving her children who'd make her smile like the rest of her healthy family?

"My best bet," Felicia said, wanting to cheer up her friends—cheer up herself—"is to find that special someone who's going to love me no matter what. Just like you all have pointed out."

"Maybe Jackson North?" Carlota smiled broadly.

Felicia's heart *tweenged* at the thought of those dark eyes of his. Soulful. Layered with experience.

"I wish he'd be interested." Felicia tried to calm the shimmer of her pulse, tried to get a hold of her common sense.

"Oh, come on," Carlota continued, "you know he's over at the Hanging R mooning over you already. You've got that immediate effect on men."

"Hanging R?" Emmy asked. "Is that where he works?"

Felicia nodded, unexplained optimism boiling, tickling her veins.

"Actually, Deston talked to Rip McCain this

week," Emmy added, the sentence coming out in a rush. "The Hanging R's definitely worse off than anyone thought. The cook quit because he hadn't been paid in weeks, and Rip hired another hand to replace the ones who've left. One *last* hand, Deston thinks."

Carlota's eyes started to saucer even before Emmy could finish.

"My husband says this new wrangler Rip's hired is the last cowboy the Hanging R will ever see."

Emmy's pronouncement sank in, burying itself into Felicia like seeds in a garden—waiting to be watered by faith and tears.

Waiting to flower.

Jack North—the last cowboy on the Hanging R?

If only Felicia could bring herself to believe in her destiny as easily as her friends did.

Chapter Three

As the next day's sun tucked itself behind the highs and lows of Texas hill country, Felicia drove to the Hanging R, got out of her used, temperamental Pontiac and clutched some grocery bags against her chest. The vibration of her heartbeat pulsed against the paper, shaking it ever so slightly.

How had Emmy and Carlota even talked her into coming over here? It was bad enough that she wanted to believe all this "last cowboy" talk. Actually showing up to see if the prediction would come true was even worse.

Still, a tiny flare of faith had been lit in her.

A dream.

Step one in Felicia's Big Plan to win over the future father of her child?

The slam of the car door caught the attention of the men on Rip McCain's buckling porch. Both cowboys had their denim-covered legs stretched out in front of them. One man—the infamous Rip McCain—swayed back and forth on a screeching swing that Felicia could hear even a hundred feet away. The other—Jack!—leaned back in a chair, taking a knife to what she guessed was a piece of wood. The glow from an inside lamp lent the pine cabin's windows a sleepy warmth, matching the orange of dusk. The structure seemed lonely resting on the desolate spread, framed by a creaky windmill, a graying barn and a bunkhouse.

The cow dog, a Queensland heeler, chugged over to greet her.

"Hey, J-Wayne," she said, wishing her hands were empty so she could pet him.

The mangy guy simply wagged his tail, giving Felicia enough courage to see if Jack had glanced up from his whittling to lay eyes on her yet.

Nope.

If he was her destiny, shouldn't it be easier to attract him?

Old Rip, the owner and ranch foreman of the Hanging R, stuck up his arm in greeting and creaked down the steps toward her. He walked as if he'd been riding a horse for all his years and had just now climbed down.

One more glance told her that Jack was still absorbed in his work. Great.

"Hello, there, little Markowski," Rip said, rubbing his hands together. His hat was tilted back, revealing silver stubble and sun-leathered skin. He talked around a bump in the bottom of his lip. Snuff. "What have we here?"

He was more subdued than usual. Was it because of the failing ranch? Or...yeah, more likely it had to do with the impending arrival of Rip's great-nephew, a boy he'd never met. County gossip held that Rip hadn't even seen his nephew's parents since they'd been kids, yet he'd been the only remaining relative who was able to take the six-year-old in.

Good old Rip. Salt of the earth.

Felicia hitched up the bags as they slipped from her grasp. "I'm done with housekeeping for the day, so I volunteered to be neighborly, seeing as you're short a cook."

"Aw, his brisket was tough anyway."

Neither of them mentioned why the unpaid employee had left the Hanging R.

He relieved her of both bags, and J-Wayne pattered away from them, heading off to sniff at her car.

"So how're you, Rip?"

"Happier than a lost soul with hell in a flood," he said.

Though she wasn't sure what that meant, his grin told her that something as minor as bankruptcy wasn't about to get him down.

"Aside from the fund-raiser, I haven't seen you around for a couple of months," she said, walking next to him as they headed for the porch.

"Been busy keepin' busy here."

Out of the corner of her eye, she kept track of Jack North. Maybe Carlota had been wrong about him giving her a baby. If he was her true love, then why hadn't the man paid her any mind since she'd driven up the Hanging R's drive?

He's going to make you a mother.

She could almost feel the tender weight of a baby's sleeping body curled in her arms. She'd held a hundred younger cousins and they'd all tugged at her heartstrings.

But cuddling a body that had slept inside *hers?* One that had been nourished by her love?

Felicia held back a rush of need. God in heaven, all she wanted was that child.

And a man who could just love her, even if she couldn't manage to give him the baby she longed to have.

Had she only been imagining the way Jack had

looked at her during the charity event? Could he ever find her attractive—outside *and* in?

"Jackson!" Rip was halfway up the cabin steps. "Company calls. Or does that there wood provide better conversation?"

If her blood had been skipping through her body thirty seconds ago, it was sprinting now.

The wrangler's hat hid the weathered face that had haunted last night's dreams. Even today, while she'd worked with the other maids dusting and polishing Oakvale's massive bedrooms, she'd been dizzy with his image.

Curled shavings gathered around Jack's feet, withered and forgotten. "Wood doesn't make unnecessary small talk," he said. "That's for certain."

Oh. Had that been some sort of dig about how she couldn't keep her mouth shut yesterday?

He wasn't so happy to see her here, was he?

Though he still whittled away, Felicia could see that the stick wasn't taking any sort of shape. Rip shrugged at her and opened the cabin's door. The hinges yelped as he went in.

Silence, except for the dry whisper of blade on wood.

"Hi, Jack," she said.

Whisk. He finally looked up at her, squinting against the waning light of day. If she didn't know better, she would have guessed that it actually pained him to see her.

"I guess that's how it is around here," he said, resting his elbows on his thighs. "Neighbors always dropping by with grub and good intentions."

Her first instinct was to defend the care packages against the word *grub.* Not that she was about to announce that Emmy had spent hours helping her prepare that *grub,* but with the way he just sort of spat it out, he sure didn't sound grateful.

"You don't get hungry like the rest of us?" she asked playfully.

Slay them with kindness—that's what she always said. She'd win him over, all right.

Jack squinted even harder and shook his head. "Didn't mean to offend. I'm not big on unexpected company, is all."

A hearty "whoo-hoo!" sounded from inside the cabin. Rip had probably found Emmy's chocolate-dipped cherries.

Felicia leaned against the skeletal porch railing, but it let out a groan of protest, so she decided to sit on Rip's swing instead. The sounds it made weren't much more reassuring.

"Wycliffe," she said, "is a community. Almost a family. When someone's sick, we come running. When someone's down and out, we offer our hand

and hope they grab on. If you're going to live here, you'd better get used to company."

His spine seemed to stiffen under his shirt. "Don't get me wrong, Ms. Markowski—"

"Felicia. I'm named after my grandmother—"

"—but when I hired on here, I just wanted a place where I could plant my bones. By myself. Except for Rip, of course, who yammers enough for the both of us."

"You really don't enjoy getting to know other people?"

Slice. Back to whittling. "After so many years, there's not much of a need."

Oh.

Unchecked, she blurted out her next question. "What the heck made you so standoffish?"

The knife blade stopped in midair, floating above the wood.

"I'm sorry," she said. "You don't know me well enough to answer."

Yet.

He snapped the knife back into itself, then slowly lay the malformed stick on the porch boards next to his chair. "Just so there's no mistake, don't ever expect an answer to that."

As he stood, Felicia felt more alone than she ever had. But she couldn't let him off the hook. Not when so much was at stake for her.

She got to her feet, also. Why? She wasn't sure. Was she going to tackle him in order to keep him here? Was she going to sit on him, keeping him captive, and put it all out on the line?

You're not going to believe this, but you might be a big part of my future. There's no way I'm going to give up on the possibility this easily.

Rip spoke from behind the screen door. "We've got a feast, Jackson, compliments of the lovely ladies over at Oakvale. Told you there were benefits to working at the Hanging R. Good eating is only the beginning. Get in here."

Jack merely adjusted his hat and slipped a gaze Felicia's way, hooking his thumbs in the back pockets of his jeans.

The sun angled over his tall, rope-muscled body, shading half his face in darkness while the other half remained soulfully weary.

Looking at him, Felicia lost the ability to stand up straight. Her stomach twisted with pent-up longing. A sweet lightness tingled the area around her heart, cradling it with care.

Some would call her ridiculous, but she didn't know what it was about Jack North. The man was cranky, didn't reveal a thing about himself and had the gall to make her feel unwelcome, yet…

Hmm. Was it because he was mysterious? A challenge of sorts?

Rip's amused voice broke the moment wide open. "You two going to eat or not? We've got some pies, fancy stew and breads…."

Thank you, Emmy, Felicia thought.

"You want me to stay?" she asked.

Jack shuffled his boots.

"You're our privileged guest." Rip motioned her inside. His wiry body didn't seem much bigger than a fence pole, but he was just as sturdy.

Jack spoke up. "Let her go, Rip."

So he really didn't want her around—not now, at least. Could she win him bit by bit? Jack North obviously wasn't a man who took to being forced into a situation. Time was all he needed to get used to the fact that he could be meant for her.

And she was looking forward to convincing him, too.

Warmed by the thought, Felicia made her way down the steps, keeping that smile on her face. Maybe she'd lost the battle, but she'd win the war.

"Really, Rip," she said. "Enjoy the spoils. The calzones are particularly good."

"Cal-what?"

She laughed. "I'll see you."

As she walked away, she tossed one last grin over her shoulder—

—and caught Jack North watching her go, eyes barely visible beneath the brim of his hat.

Bang! Her heart thudded against her ribs, blood thundering through her body.

Well, now. What about that.

Her steps lightened in time to the cadence of Rip's thank-yous and farewells. As she prepared to leave, she couldn't help humming to herself.

Maybe the world would be her oyster. The sun would come out tomorrow. The…

The car wasn't starting.

She tried again. And again.

Maybe she was meant to stay for dinner, after all.

"Good cookin'," Rip repeated for about the one hundredth time as the three of them sat at the small dinner table. "Too bad the other hands went to town tonight. Poor pokes."

Jackson had his mouth full of some fancy cinnamon bread, so it gave him an excuse not to engage. Needless to say, as Rip had waxed splendiferous about Felicia's chow and the woman herself had made pleasant chatter, Jackson had been doing a lot of gourd stuffing.

He found himself watching her throughout the meal, chastising his body every time he caught himself doing it.

When she'd first gotten out of the car, Rip had let loose some remark about Felicia being the first woman in a flood of females to come and claim his new wrangler. Jackson hoped to God there wouldn't be any more.

Felicia was enough.

Now, her summer-shine hair was tucked behind her ears, sheeting down her back. And she did have a cute little tipped-up nose to go along with those bright eyes. She reminded Jackson of one of the barn kittens—spirited, open-faced, innocent.

Hell. He'd already spent his last chance at happiness. Now, all he wanted to do was ride his mount over the country, communicating with a mere squeeze of his legs as he sat in the saddle. No more words.

No more blame.

Just him and the silent days ahead.

Rip was laughing—or wheezing, Jackson wasn't sure which—at something Felicia had said. She'd thrown back her head in amusement, too, throat exposed, dimples framing her smile.

"Aw." Rip sighed and patted his stomach. "I never could stand that other boy's cookin', and mine ain't much better. Not that we have the time or energy to work the kitchen after a long day anyway."

He jerked his stubbled chin in Jackson's direction. In answer, Jackson merely shrugged and drew back into himself, making sure Felicia didn't know that his mouth had been going dry at the sight of her.

"So what do you usually eat?" she asked.

"Whatever the ladies bring round." Rip's expression turned sly. "I expect a whole lot of gourmet offerings with the playboy bachelor here."

Felicia blushed furiously, which made Jackson steam.

"Pipe down, Rip."

"Is it some secret that you're a single man? I could live like a king if you set your mind to working your wiles on the ladies of Wycliffe."

Fighting a grin, Felicia said, "You've got a pretty blunt boss, Jack."

You could say the same about my fist filling his mouth, Jackson thought. Pretty damned blunt, too.

"Don't worry," she continued. "Rip's right about there being a lot of willing ladies in the area, but they won't bother you as soon as they hear you don't encourage the companionship."

Hallelujah, she'd finally caught on.

Was it time to hit the bunkhouse yet? The clock above the sink said eight o'clock. Damn.

"Tell me, Little Markowski," Rip said, "do all the women in your family work a pan so good?"

Her mouth moved, but then she shut it. Then she began, "I, uh…"

Rip forged ahead. "Because we could sure use a cook until someone permanent comes along. Yup, we could use a dough puncher like you. Couldn't we, Jackson?"

The old man chuckled, taking great pleasure in his employee's mortification. The boss knew how to push his buttons, that was for certain.

Jackson just sank lower in his chair. All he needed was Felicia around to drive him to distraction.

"I already have a job, remember?" she said. "Over at Oakvale?"

That's right. She didn't have time for these childish games. So much for Rip's bright ideas.

"Can't say I didn't try." Rip winked at her and stood, gathering his crumb-littered plate, but Jackson still caught the twist of despair in the old cowboy's gaze.

Following his boss's progress toward the sink, Jackson's brow furrowed. Rip moved like his joints needed a good greasing, and he held himself up by using the counter as he stared out the window at the darkness.

During the fund-raiser, Felicia had talked about the ranch's poor state. Truth to tell, Jackson had been concerned, too, and not only about finances.

The boy was coming soon. Bobby. More than just another mouth to feed.

Jackson actually panicked at a name that would soon go with a small, all-too-real face.

When Rip turned back around from the sink, he nonetheless had that ever-present lump pushing out his bottom lip, tobacco or not. His eyes glittered, a teasing shade of blue, much like Felicia's.

Jackson's pulse popped just thinking about their shine.

She had an intense quirk to her eyebrows while scrutinizing Rip. "Is there anything I can do to—"

"We're right as rain," he said, cutting her off. "Don't you worry about the Hanging R."

The thoughtful expression remained on her face as her eyes met Jackson's, as if needing him to second Rip's positive outlook.

Jackson lowered his gaze, stung by the heat thrashing under his skin.

Before he'd gotten divorced, Jenna, his ex-wife, had looked to him for solace in times of need. For opinions, as if he could take care of everything. They'd both learned the hard way that he wasn't capable of much.

He was real good at damage, and that was about it.

"Rip…?" Felicia asked.

The old man clapped together his hands, grabbed his hat and headed for the door in a show of avoidance. "I told you I'd take a gander at that Pontiac to see what the problem is. Here I go."

And with that, he left them alone in the dimly lit kitchen, the red-and-white gingham tablecloth being the loudest object in the room.

Felicia leaned her elbow on the table and her hair spilled over her arm. "Be straight with me. Is he taking on too much with this ranch and now his nephew?"

Jackson shifted in his chair. He himself wasn't even ready for Bobby to be here. The thought of having a child around the age of Leroy and Lucas, who were frozen in his memory as eternal little boys, tore him apart.

"You know Old Rip. He loves taking in strays. He'll be all right." Especially since Bobby was coming to them with enough money from his late parents to cover his living expenses, for a while, at least.

"I don't understand how he'll take care of a boy and labor like he does." She paused, then her eyes lit up. "You know, I'll bet my friend Emmy and her husband Deston could improve matters. They wouldn't hesitate to lend some money or help."

"Wait, now. I haven't known Rip that long, but I'm pretty certain he won't accept charity. Seems stubborn as a jackass."

"But look at this place." Felicia motioned around, her eyes having gone softhearted, her hair shifting position and sliding against a shoulder. "He can't refuse. Besides, maybe I could talk him into accepting…a loan."

A curse word bucked against Jackson's teeth, dying to get out. This girl was naive enough to break stone into pieces.

And, somehow, that got to him.

"Stay out of the man's business." The words ground out of him. Too gruff. Too harsh.

Her lips parted as she blinked. "I only want to help."

"I know you do."

And those words had come out too quietly, an opening he couldn't close back up. A half-healed wound stretched apart—raw and unprotected once again.

Abruptly, he shoved back his chair, stood, grabbed a plate and headed toward that convenient sink. Couldn't she just go home and leave them alone? Who needed a do-gooder around?

He could feel her sitting there, watching his back. Every move he made ached, felt cold and unnatural.

"Jack?"

Her voice sounded unsure. He fought the urge to turn around and lay a hand against her jaw, allowing his thumb to linger against her cheek in apology.

"Yeah?" he asked.

"Can you just look at me for once?"

He didn't owe her anything. Not like he owed Jenna or their boys.

There was only so much of himself he could give, whether it was in charitable glances or penance.

Still, he turned his face, almost catching her in his sights, showing her he was listening to whatever it was she wanted to say.

"I believe in honesty, so I'm going to…" Her sentence wobbled a little, like an infant taking her first steps. She exhaled, as if culling strength from the gesture. "What Rip said about women chasing after you with their food and visits?"

Silence.

She continued. "I suppose I'm one of those hopefuls."

Now, why had she gone and said something like that?

A thrust of emotion forced him back from the sink, head down, hands grasping the steel rim to steady himself. He wished he had his hat to hide behind.

"I—" she said.

"Don't say any more."

She didn't.

He tried to gather his confusion into one place inside of himself, to stuff it where no one could find it again.

Finally, he stiffened his spine, took advantage of the roar of Rip's pickup engine as it revved outside the door.

"I'm not the sort of man who revels in the attention," he managed to say.

"Why not?"

When he chanced a look at her, his gut tightened into a fist of heat. She was a sweet one, all right. But he didn't have the energy for living through more heartbreak. Six years of drifting from ranch to ranch was the only thing that had sustained him, kept him alive.

He wouldn't ever settle anywhere because that's when the pain would catch up.

"Why not?" he repeated. "Because you probably have a line of guys waiting for you to crook your finger at them. Because I'm too wrung out to keep up with you. There're a million becauses, but don't think I'm not flattered."

"I didn't come here to flatter you, Jack North."

"You'll get over me. Real quick. Believe it."

"We'll see about that." Her smile returned full force, as if she was remembering something. His knees about buckled.

What did she mean? They'd known each other one day, and already she was crazy about him? Damn, she was inexperienced, forward...

...and foolish.

The clunk of Rip's boots as he climbed the outside steps put a cap on the conversation, thank heavens. The old man cracked open the door.

"Your ride just needs a jump. You ready?" he asked Felicia.

She angled her head toward Jackson, that smile stretching over her lips, bathing her face in growing confidence.

"I think I'm ready," she answered, getting out of her seat. "Ready for anything."

At that moment, Jackson knew he was in some deep trouble. Wheels were turning behind that sparkling blue gaze. She'd decided on something and he hated to guess just what it was.

As she left, she flittered her fingers in a small wave, forcing Jackson to grasp the counter for balance again.

Long after she'd left, he was still watching the door.

Chapter Four

Felicia had gotten to Jack, no doubt about that.

When she'd told him that she wanted to come around and see him again—hadn't *that* taken some guts?—the stubborn guy had softened toward her, had tried to let her down easy.

But seeing him again had only recharged her, convincing her that Carlota's prediction could indeed come true with a little extra nudge here and there.

And that's why she'd talked to Emmy and Deston when she'd gotten home from the Hanging R.

As expected, they'd agreed to arrange it so Felicia could be "loaned out" to Rip for the time being, taking care of his household until a permanent cook could be found.

It was the neighborly thing to do. Heh heh.

But, strangely enough, Carlota hadn't been quite as sold on the idea.

"You've decided you're going to cook for Rip?" she'd asked, making what Felicia and Emmy called the you've-got-to-be-messin'-with-me face. "I mean, I appreciate what you're trying to do here, but…cooking?"

"He needs help."

"*You're* cooking. *You.*"

"I can cook."

"You *want* to cook, Felicia. You collect recipes and fantasize about throwing dinner parties, but you never actually do it."

"That doesn't mean I can't."

"I know, it's just…" Carlota had tossed up her hands. "I was thinking that since Jackson North is your destiny, maybe he could just come to you."

And they called Felicia an optimist.

She'd ignored Carlota's doubts and forged ahead, making arrangements with Rip, who could barely contain his excitement at having "a woman's touch" in the cabin. Further preparing herself, she pumped Emmy for hints about fixing more than microwave dinners or her favorite dinnertime meal—cheese and tomato sandwiches.

Cooking. She could pull this off. No problem.

Her plan was simple and would therefore work: take care of Rip while getting to Jack North the best way a woman could.

Through his stomach.

She didn't see how it could go wrong.

The next day, in the Hanging R's kitchen, Felicia found herself choking on smoke from a hank of burned pan-fried steak.

She wasn't going to call Emmy again. Nope. Wouldn't happen.

A flare of warm, char-tinged wind from the opened window over the sink belled the gingham curtains and whooshed into her face. Coughing, she tried to wave the stench away.

It'd all gone so well at first. Rip and the hands had been checking the fences today, so she'd made herself at home in the cabin. Rip had insisted that she stay here while he moved to the bunkhouse with the other men. After resisting—she hated putting people out of their beds—she'd realized this was a matter of pride for the rancher. He wanted to treat her like a "lady," giving her separate, superior quarters. After all, he'd reminded her, he wouldn't be able to pay her right away and he wanted to make up for the trouble.

Felicia didn't actually intend to accept any wages from Rip McCain, but she hadn't argued. Instead, she'd set about starting dinner. This morning, before she'd arrived, the men had packed themselves lunch and a canteen to keep them satisfied on the go, but it was up to her to have a decent meal ready when they returned tonight.

Decent meal. She'd be lucky if the cabin was still standing by the time they got back.

When she finally gave in and dialed Emmy for the fourth time that day, her friend couldn't hide her worry.

"You're in over your head."

"Don't sound like Carlota." Felicia coughed a little, but then the wind changed direction, and the smoke veered away. See? Everything would be fine. Even the weather had decided to help. "I've got something that resembles sourdough biscuits ready and waiting, but the stove could be cooperating more, and I'm nervous about burning all the steaks."

"If I weren't overseeing the restaurant tonight, I'd be there helping you."

Emmy owned a chic eatery in San Antonio featuring Tuscan cuisine. Even though she was wealthy now that she'd married Deston, she still insisted on working the kitchens every so often, when she wasn't taking care of Nigel.

"Em, don't you dare fret about me. I've got beef, beans, potatoes, biscuits, coffee and your apple crisp to keep these boys full. And thanks for dessert, by the way. I couldn't help sampling."

"Anything for you, darlin'."

Distracted by the burbling beans on the stovetop, Felicia initiated their goodbyes. Then she turned off the cell phone and set it on the faded windowsill, thinking no more about it.

The day was waning and Rip's instructions said the men would be back around sundown. So, knowing this, Felicia went step-by-step through the notes she'd taken for Emmy's steak preparation, making sure she would fry them well-done in a cast-iron skillet and sprinkle flour into the beef grease to brown up a thick gravy for the biscuits.

Soon, Felicia heard the men guiding their horses toward the barn, J-Wayne the cow dog nipping at the animals' heels.

Felicia tried to concentrate on the cooking, but she found herself seeking Jack through the window, anticipating the easy sway of his body as he rode his quarter horse.

It'd been too long since she'd last seen him—not since the night she'd visited the Hanging R. And…okay, it'd only been the night before last. She wasn't proud to admit she craved being around him so much.

But even though she wanted to spend as much time as possible with Jack, she knew knocking him over the head with her presence would do no good. He'd made that more than clear. But at least she had an excuse to be here. Contributing. Working for a good cause.

She looked down at another slab of blackened meat—a victim of her daydreaming.

So what exactly was she contributing? Ashes?

The bungled steak disappeared amid aluminum foil and assorted trash that she stored in a bag underneath the sink. She would do a better job of hiding her mistakes later.

In the meantime, she turned on Rip's old-fashioned, turbine-looking, dust-furred, high-power fan. After wiping it down, of course. Boy, she sure had her cleaning work cut out for her.

Mood lifted by the return of Jack, she set about cooking the next steak, which ended up—yes, thank you!—*perfect*.

Or close enough.

After the men had cleaned up in the bunkhouse, they gathered at a long oak table near the porch outside, and Felicia welcomed them by delivering the food. Once she set the dishes down, they greedily shoveled "grub" onto their plates, then waited for Rip and Jack to arrive. Soon, the old man limped out of the bunkhouse, his mouth tight with the pain he was no doubt trying to cover.

While Felicia just about jumped out of her skin wondering where Jack was, she watched Rip settle. What could she do to make him feel better? She put her mind to it.

She also kept an eye on the men's faces, hoping she'd done a good job with the hash slinging.

Shoot, *where was Jack?*

Rip took a bite of the beans, to which she'd added brown sugar, bacon and onions. Too bad there was an extra element of burned matter in the mix, but all in all, she was happy with how they'd turned out.

"Music to my innards," Rip said, shaking his fork in the air with emphasis.

One of the hands, Dutch, bunched up his withered face as he tried to bite into a biscuit. Then he glanced at her apologetically. "I like a lot of gravy anyway," he said, enthusiastically dipping it so the bread would loosen up.

They weren't saying much, just chowing down, so Felicia took that as a good sign. She crept toward the cabin, intending to make a secret phone call to Emmy and tell her all was well.

Once inside, she checked the windowsill for her phone. Not finding it, she riffled through a shoulder bag that she'd plopped on the kitchen table, but the cell wasn't there. Well. Had she been so busy that she'd lost it?

"Looking for this?" a low, rusted voice said from the direction of the back door.

Felicia jumped, startled to find Jack, who was shadowed by the door's screen. He doffed his hat and pushed the screen open, the hinges whining.

He hadn't grabbed his meal yet, so there wasn't much excuse for the frown lining his face.

Welcome to the Hanging R, Felicia.

His black eyes dug into her as he tossed his hat on a kitchen chair and held out her cell phone. Whoops. It'd dropped off the windowsill and onto the ground, hadn't it?

And why was he looking at her like that? Because he suspected she couldn't work an oven without dialing help? Heck, she'd cooked dinner on her own. Almost.

As a matter of fact, she could accomplish any piece of so-called feminine work. She could be all woman, no matter what anyone else said.

Sticking out her palm, she walked toward him and tacitly asked for the phone.

Surprisingly, he smiled—if you could call this rough approximation such a thing. The sight of it melted her heart. And when she got even closer, she just about sighed in appreciation.

His tanned skin. The strong line of his bristled jaw.

Wow.

Her fingers brushed his as she reached out and grasped the phone.

A lick of breath-stealing flame singed her and he jerked away, stuffing both hands in his jeans pockets.

Her skin tingled, wavered like heat patterns inside a burning piece of wood. She pressed a finger against the vibration of his touch on her hand, feeling the spread of desire soaking through the rest of her body.

Being this close to Jack North did crazy things to her. *Nice,* crazy things.

"Thank you," she said.

"I thought we hashed out matters the other night," he said, watching her from beneath a lowered brow. "I didn't expect to see you around here again."

"What exactly did we hash out?" she asked with a perky grin. "Remind me."

Jackson was almost sorry to sound so accusatory, but how else could he act with his body betraying his better instincts? One little slide of her finger against his had thrown him into a dither, and the loss of control spooked him.

His ribs squeezed together, protecting whatever was sleeping inside.

"I thought I told you that I don't need the company."

"Oh." She stared at him as if trying to decipher what he'd just said. Then she smiled in understanding, threw her head back in a laugh.

Was he wrong? Based on what she'd confessed the other night, wasn't she here pretty much to court him or…whatever you wanted to call it?

Jackson's face got hot with embarrassment.

"Jack," she said, propping her hands on her

curvy, jeans-encased hips, "first and foremost, I'm here for Rip."

Her smile told him that she wanted to say more, that she was here to be around him, too, but he stopped her.

"Please don't tell me you're out to save him from destitution."

"Then I won't." She accompanied her shrug with a cute purse of the lips.

"Listen, Ms. Markowski—"

"Felicia. There are seven of us in the area, named after—"

"I know, I was listening the first time. You're named after your grandma."

She raised her eyebrows, probably because he'd recalled this personal detail. Hell, he was just as stunned, too.

He found himself fighting a grin. Why? Who knew. It's just that Felicia Markowski brought out something in him—made him want to peek out of his self-imposed shell and make plenty of excuses about why he should be doing it.

It scared him to death, kind of.

He glanced down at the floor, forcing himself to get serious again.

"I like the fired-up version of you, Jack," she said. "You've got some spunk when you put your mind to it."

"As I was saying," he enunciated slowly, trying not to give in to that tiny speck of amusement in him that was growing by the second, "this kitchen reeks of smoke, and don't tell me you're cooking Cajun. These men need to eat healthy to stay fit for work. Food's not something to trifle with after a long, hard day."

He glanced up in time to see her making a dismissive motion with her hand.

"Look outside, they're stuffing themselves. I think I did pretty okay. And wait until you see dessert."

Jackson's guard slipped. He'd caught a whiff of something sweet in the air. Something that hung over the sting of burned meat.

He had a goody fixation like no other. Any mention of junk food broke him down.

"What kind of dessert?" he asked.

"Apple crisp with just a hint of orange in it. So good your taste buds will do the cancan."

He sniffed the air, this time almost tasting the fruit and sugar. His mouth started to water.

"It'll do," he said, a mammoth growl building in his belly.

"Wonderful. There'll be no more complaints from you tonight, I suppose."

She flashed him an expression that was half smug, half teasing, and Jackson felt like more of a heel than ever. Two minutes ago he'd been on her case about not taking her new duties seriously, and now he was her apple crisp slave.

What was it about her that convinced him he needed to lighten up?

At any rate, maybe an apology was in order. "Listen—"

He reached out and brushed her upper arm, hardly realizing what he was doing. The gesture was left over from the days when conversation had been more a part of his life: a hand on the shoulder of his wife while they discussed the boys' futures. A pat on the back when Leroy or Lucas experienced a down day.

But recently, reaching out was so damned unlike him that he couldn't help correcting himself, barring both arms over his chest to prevent another accidental touch.

Still, as Felicia tilted her head and encouraged him with a gentle gaze, he could feel the memory of the soft shape of her arm on the tips of his fingers. Unable to help himself, his imagination took over from there, conjuring guesses as to how her skin would look while bathed outside in this darkening light, how her mouth would curve if he ran his hands all over her body—traveling it, worshipping it.

He spoke, just to regain his mental balance, his arms tight against his body. "I'm sorry about being such a hard case. I just want to make sure everything goes smooth for Rip."

"You're a good friend," she said softly. "Rip's lucky to have hired someone who looks out for him like you do."

While he paused, Felicia's hand floated up to coast over her arm, over the area he'd touched. The reminder of the intimate accident made him go hot in the face, all over his body. The innocence of her movement couldn't have been more seductive, laying him bare because he wanted to do it one more time.

Wanted to do so much more.

He started to walk toward the front door, running away yet again, but her voice stopped him.

"I have a confession."

The low song of her tone slowed him down, turned him around.

She shrugged, pointed toward the oven. "The crisp? I didn't make it. My friend Emmylou Rhodes is a real fine chef and she sent it over with me today. I only warmed the dessert up."

A flush stained her cheeks and he could guess that she hadn't wanted to let this particular cat out of the bag.

Had she wanted to impress him that much?

"But," she added, "I really *can* cook. I just need a flexing period, like a ballet dancer."

She sounded so sincere, so well-meaning.

In fact, it looked as if her soul were in her eyes, reaching out to him, trying to convince him to step over the line he'd drawn years ago. To give up and allow her in.

"I'll—" he motioned toward the front door "—be outside. Eating." He turned back around then walked a step or two. Stopped. "Your food. Eating your food."

Now, that awkwardness had been prizeworthy.

Leaving well enough alone, Jackson retrieved his hat, then drew it down over his eyes as he made his way to the table with the other wranglers.

He never even glanced back at Felicia.

Looking back would hurt too much either way.

As Felicia began to collect the gravy-sopped plates from the outside table, the men stoked a fire in a cement ring, gathering around the night heat to relax.

"Leave that for later," Rip said, emptying her hands. "Dishes can always be cleaned, but the stars are right beautiful at this moment."

One peek at the crowd around the fire assured Felicia that Jack hadn't gone to the bunkhouse. She was shocked that he hadn't burned rubber out of her sight yet, what with the way he'd actually opened up to her in the kitchen.

Opened up being a relative term, of course. But,

for Jack North, that touch on her arm had been akin to a nationally televised speech.

While Rip hobbled to the fire, she took a second to relive the dizzy moment—in slow motion, even.

Jack with the hint of a grin.

Jack loosening up.

Jack's hand rising, coming closer, meeting the skin of her upper arm.

Jack looking horrified.

She'd just as soon forget that last part because it didn't fit too well with the fantasy. But at least the other images would keep her going until morning.

Progress! Tonight, fleeting contact. Tomorrow…?

When she sat on one of the tattered lawn chairs, the men welcomed her. The wrangler named Carter had even pulled out a harmonica and he was working on some tune Felicia didn't recognize.

Rip patted her knee. "Carter's learnin', and we're toleratin'."

The men chuckled—even Jack.

Now, why was it so hard for *her* to get a laugh out of him?

She noticed that he was sitting far away from the flames, a part of the group without actually being in the midst of it. He was even facing away from the fire, as if pretending it wasn't there.

"At the risk of sounding like an ingrate in the face of such accomplished music," said a cowboy named Stoverson, a man who sat straighter than the rest of the workers and had a deep, oddly cultured voice, "I'd like to hear Ms. Markowski's story."

"That's right," Dutch said. "We all go through it when we're hired on. Campfire introductions. A rite of passage."

If possible, this wrangler's skin was in even worse shape than Rip's. Not that Dutch was ancient; he just hadn't aged gracefully.

"Then, Ms. Markowski," Rip said, "it looks like it's your night to entertain us."

She thought she saw Jack's shoulders rise in slight laughter as he reached into his jeans pockets then brought out the switchblade and a fresh stick of wood.

Snick, snick, went his whittling.

"I'm not all that interesting," she said. "Unless you want to gossip about the Rhodes family."

Dutch leaned closer and Carter set down his harmonica.

"Is it true," Stoverson said, "that one of the sons married a maid and leveled a stroke on big Mr. Rhodes after it was all said and done?"

"The cook," Felicia said. "Deston married the cook. Emmylou's one of my best friends. And as for Mr. Rhodes's stroke, Deston didn't eventually bring it on as much as lots of eating, smoking and working did."

Dutch flipped a cigarette into his mouth, lit it to life. "I hear everyone on Oakvale has to take medical classes now," he said around the smoking stick, "in case Mr. Rhodes has another attack."

Felicia shook her head at the exaggeration. "Mrs. Rhodes has us trained in CPR, and there's a nurse on the premises. It's just a matter of caution, just in case any of us happen upon him at a bad moment."

Yes, maybe it did sound like overkill, but Felicia would go any distance for her employers. She would even learn to do open heart surgery to keep Mr. Rhodes safe, if it came right down to it.

Carter and Dutch tripped all over each other, asking more questions, immediately tagging themselves as the gossip hounds of the group. But Felicia swerved the talk away from the Rhodes family's personal matters and kept up her end of the campfire bargain by offering anecdotes about her massive family: stories about her great-great-grandparents settling here, her mother and father defying the wishes of their parents and marrying outside of their ethnicities, the tradition of working on the Rhodeses' estate for the women of her family.

It occurred to Felicia that she was performing for Jack, trying in a roundabout way to bridge the gap between the two of them, using bystanders as go-betweens.

"I saw all those cousins running around Oakvale," Rip said. "Hundreds of them. Good-looking rug rats. Is your family aiming to take over the county? Are you all going to breed until there's no room for anyone else?"

Even though Rip was joking, the comments sliced through her.

When she hesitated, too distracted to answer, Jack glanced up, their gazes connecting.

For a heartbeat, he looked into her, hard features gentling. Searching.

Had he somehow heard about her problems? Was that why he was already so standoffish, because he didn't want to start anything with a woman who couldn't follow through with the promises her gender was born to make?

This time, Felicia was the one who broke eye contact, standing, brushing off her jeans just to give herself something to do.

"Those dishes aren't going to wash themselves," she said. "You boys have fun."

They tried to convince her to stay, but she couldn't.

Not with Jack still gauging her.

Chapter Five

The next morning, after Felicia had served up fried eggs, beef, potatoes, fruit, coffee and juice, the men went their separate ways: Dutch and Carter were fixing the water tank floats in the corrals while Jack and Stoverson made a trip to Wycliffe to buy fencing posts and wire for repairs. Rip had traveled with them in order to see a lawyer about the final legal paperwork for guardianship of Bobby, whose arrival was just around the corner.

Before all three of them had piled into the pickup's cab, Rip had found Felicia wearing long rubber gloves and taking a scrub brush to the nooks and crannies of his kitchen.

"This shack'll be brand spankin' new if you're not careful," he said, leaning against a chair.

Felicia rested her hands on her thighs, unmindful of the dirt she was getting on her work jeans. "I'll be sure to leave a few spiderwebs and dust bunnies, just to keep this place feeling like home."

"That's the spirit."

Usually, Rip delivered his conversation with more spunk. What was going on with him?

"Anxious about Bobby?" she asked.

"Hell, yeah." He exhaled, seemingly relieved that she'd guessed. "I'm an ancient bachelor. Never had more than a dog for a pet, not countin' the horses and beeves, of course. But that's not the same, is it?"

"You're willing to give him a home. That counts more than anything."

"Let's hope." He started to leave, then shot her a sheepish glance. "Say, you got the fixin's to make more of that apple stuff tonight?"

Had Jack told Rip about Felicia's culinary deception? That she wasn't exactly a crisp queen?

"Anything you want," Felicia said, determined to whip up the best treat they'd ever tasted. "And I'll have lunch ready for everyone, to boot."

Rip sighed, patting his flat stomach. "What did I do to deserve you, little Markowski?"

"You must've lived a good life at some point."

After the rancher took his leave, she shone up the kitchen to her satisfaction, then set to work on the food. Emmy and she had raided the Oakvale pantries, so there was no shortage of cooking supplies.

She'd also made copies of Emmy's favorite recipes; the apple crisp was indeed among them.

And she was off, determined to make mouths water and tummies groan with pleasure—especially since she'd seen how much Jack had enjoyed the aroma of Emmy's baking yesterday.

Felicia wanted him to feel the same way about *her* cooking. It was silly, really, possessive and competitive, but she wanted to give Jack something she'd made with affection.

Something she'd produced herself.

Following Emmy's directions—and even adding some coconut flakes that she found in the Oakvale pantry supplies—Felicia mixed the ingredients, then baked her buns off.

When noon rolled around, she'd swarmed the cabin with the aroma of homemade goods. The crisp—and lunch—had turned out beautifully.

She *could* be of use in the kitchen, doggonit.

As she served the lasagna outside at the long table—sure, it wasn't the most challenging of dishes, but she'd done it without messing up—even Jack seemed to like it. He gave her a slow nod, then shoveled the cheese and pasta into his mouth, looking for all the world like a man who hadn't eaten in years.

It was the best compliment she could have hoped for.

So he'd been wrong about Felicia, Jackson thought, savoring the final bite of his favorite Italian dish. Definitely way off the mark.

She really was serious about keeping them all well fed.

While Rip and the wranglers stretched out of their seats then wandered back to work, Jackson took a moment, rested his elbows on the rough table and lifted a cup of coffee to his lips, keeping Felicia in his sights as she collected the dishes.

Even in threadbare jeans and a faded red sleeveless shirt, she was something to behold. She'd pinned up the light strands of her hair so the pale column of her neck was exposed, damp curlicues clinging to her nape.

He imagined stirring one of the locks with a finger, allowing the caress to travel forward to her throat. Once there, he would stroke her skin, gently, easing her—and himself—into a kiss.

A soft, uninhibited kiss.

Heat invaded him at the thought of his lips whispering over hers, his fingertips skimming over her collarbone, then her chest....

"Can I take your plate?"

It was her voice, shaking him into the here and now. She was standing behind him, loaded down with dishes piled on top of one another.

Even though he itched to ask her if she needed help, he stayed seated, afraid to stand up. To find himself weak-kneed or, worse, tent-poled in the zipper area.

When would his body ever grow up? You would think he was thirteen again with the way it was acting.

"I'll clear the rest of the table in a second," he said. Once again, he sounded too damned gruff so, on a lighter note, he added, "Thanks."

"No, thank *you.*"

As she whisked by on her way to the cabin, her fragrance swept over him. A sunny day in a meadow. Butterflies, long grass and not a care in the world.

He wished he could feel that way beyond a sniff of perfume.

He watched her walk up the porch steps, carefully balancing her load, her curvy hips swiveling under jeans that hugged her rear end.

Running a hand over his face, he cut off his own view, made sure he was put together well enough to greet the public, then stood. He cleared the rest of the table, taking his time.

When Jackson finally entered the cabin, composed as ever, she was already elbow deep in sink suds.

She seemed to sense him behind her and glanced over her shoulder, arms still submerged.

Great. He was on her radar.

And damned if he didn't find himself sort of happy about that.

"There he is," she said with enough pep to convince him that they hadn't seen each other for the last year. "You can put your cargo down."

She indicated an open space of counter with her chin, and he complied, dishes clattering.

"So what are you doing for the rest of the day?" she asked.

He couldn't tolerate just standing there, so he scraped the plate remainders into the trash. Not that he meant to show her they had some sort of truce going on. He still wasn't comfortable with her around, but he didn't want to be a layabout while she labored away, either.

"Rip's got me going over his accounts," he said, grabbing a towel and a dripping dish from the drying rack. At her inquisitive glance, he added, "I've got a business background."

And that was all he was going to offer by way of personal information. No need to go into the details of his former life: the MBA from Texas A&M, the horse-breeding venture he used to run with Jenna and had planned to pass on to Leroy and Lucas someday.

"Hope you get some good news from Rip's books, then."

Felicia deposited a few cleaned forks in the rack while he let the comment go by without a response.

Like an efficient assembly line, he took up where she left off, making quick work out of the now-spotless utensils.

It crossed his mind that they were a decent team.

Silence stretched between them. Nothing to talk about. Nothing in common.

Maybe she'd catch on that they were about as far apart as two people could be and leave it at that.

Yet, instead of pushing her agenda, she merely sent him a contented grin, acknowledging the fact that they were getting along pretty nicely without needing to yammer on.

Ironically, he rushed to correct the misconception.

"You can't tell me you're enjoying it here," he said, "hanging around with a bunch of campfire coots."

"It's not like I have a fantastic nightlife. You've been to Wycliffe. Honky-tonks aren't really my thing."

"Then how do you meet anybody? I mean…" It sounded as if he was fishing for her dating history—which he wasn't. "How do you meet…friends?"

She gave a tiny chuff, telling him she knew he wasn't interested in friend talk.

Jeez, it was true, wasn't it? He *did* want to know about Felicia's boyfriends and all the reasons a woman like her was unattached.

Without looking, she guided a plate to the rack, but he was too quick on the trigger. As he grabbed it, their fingers brushed, zinging a bolt of electricity bone deep.

An encore from last night. A second touch, as powerful as the first.

A pause shattered the space between them. Had the same jagged attraction split her apart, too?

He busied himself, clearing his throat as a preemptive strike.

"Let's see," she said, blushing slightly. "How do I meet…friends?"

Done with the dishes, she let out the water, spraying the suds away with the movable faucet head. "Setups, compliments of my relatives. Taking random classes like quilting or self-defense from the local community college. Going to rodeos or grabbing a burger at the soda shop…. How do *you* meet…friends?"

Damn, she smelled so good. "I don't."

"You should try it, Jack. It's not so bad. Of course, relationships don't always turn out so great, either, but what's life without some risk?"

It's safe, he thought. That's what it is.

He finished drying the last dish while Felicia

tidied up the kitchen. There were a couple of pies and a cooled crisp near the windowsill on a flat wire rack, and he suspected that, this time, they were all her doing.

He warmed at the realization—just a little.

"Of course," she added, her back to him, "there're times when you're plum out of luck after you take a chance. I could tell you all about my last boyfriend, but I don't think you'd want to hear."

A stab of jealousy lit through him. Boyfriend.

He *didn't* want to hear about it.

Laying his towel on the counter, he backed away.

Idiotic, that's what he was being. He had no time or inclination for getting-to-know-you talk, for clever dating conversation that would lead to a dead end.

"I'll let you get to work," he said. "I've got a lot to do, too."

"Sure." The word came out perkier than usual, but almost in a way that overcompensated, that told him she'd been put in her place.

Had the reminder of her last boyfriend gotten to her? Or was Jackson's rudeness finally too much for her to handle?

"Thanks, again," she said.

Shockingly, she didn't pursue anything more. She merely allowed him to leave without making him feel guilty about being such a pill.

So why did he stand there for a couple more seconds than he needed to?

Damned if he knew.

Damned if a fool like him would ever know.

"Can an old man ask for your help?"

Felicia sat with Rip near the campfire that night, digesting a meal of chili, sourdough biscuits and whiskey.

The other men were trading good-humored jibes over the fire, letting off steam, yet Jack wasn't one of their number. He'd already returned to Rip's study, continuing his perusal of the accounts.

Although disappointed, Felicia figured he'd probably reached his talk quota for the day anyway. After all, he'd really spent himself during their dishwashing drill earlier, right?

But…heck. Why was she so frustrated with her apparent lack of results? One step at a time to win him over, wasn't that the plan? And he was interacting with her voluntarily now. He'd even touched her without having to be roped into it.

If that wasn't progress, she didn't know what was.

"You can ask for anything, Rip," she said, palming her mug of coffee and leaning her head back on the lawn chair's rim. Crickets sang in the night and, in the near distance, oak and juniper trees rustled in a warm, light breeze.

The rancher cuffed back his hat so it revealed more of his time-grizzled face. It allowed Felicia to see that his gaze was fairly dancing with excitement.

"You and all those cousins," he said. "Are you pretty sure you know how to take care of kids?"

Of course. Bobby again. Rip was chock-full of nerves and anticipation.

"Sometimes I feel like I've helped to raise a passel of them." She smiled, the corners of her mouth weighed down, her arms feeling so bare without anyone to hold.

"Well, that's a balm," he said, "because I don't know step one. About the details, I mean. I wouldn't have accepted Bobby if I thought I couldn't raise him up just right."

She nodded, wondering where this was going.

"I want him to know he's come home," Rip continued, "so…well…I'm just gonna ask. I know you're doing a lot with the cleanin' and cookin', but, if I gave you some cash, could you stand to go into Wycliffe tomorrow? To maybe buy a thing or two for Bobby's new room so he doesn't walk into something that looks like a monk's cell? I ain't got the touch when it comes to decoratin'."

Immediately, Felicia's mind began to whir. A boy's room. Toys, games, sports equipment, race cars…

"I'd love to," she said, making the old man sink back into his chair with relief.

They talked about Bobby and what Rip already knew about him: a big Houston Astros fan, a connoisseur of dinosaur facts, a great lover of *Star Wars* spacecraft models. Felicia grew more enthusiastic by the second, made happy by the urge to nurture and comfort.

"I'll take care of everything," she said, patting Rip on a bony shoulder. "Don't worry."

"Thanks, little Markowski. A million thanks." The rancher got up from his chair, his joints creaking. "I'll talk to Jackson about driving you out there."

Her mouth opened but no words came out. Oh, boy. Jack was going to love being her chauffeur. This would be one more notch on his complain-about-Felicia belt.

Before she could croak out an argument, the rancher chuckled. Lowering his voice so the other men couldn't hear, he said, "I might be fallin' apart at the seams, but I ain't blind. Jackson'll drive you to Wycliffe. And he'll like it, too."

With a saucy wink, Rip ambled to the cabin, then disappeared inside.

At this point, if Felicia couldn't get her last cowboy to come around, maybe Rip could give him a *huge* nudge.

With Jack, she could use all the help she could get.

* * *

That night, after closing Rip's books, Jackson had dreamed of fire.

Always the same nightmare: him, chained to a theater chair in an audience of two. His ex-wife, sitting next to him and applauding as a crimson velvet curtain parted. Onstage rested a TV set, its face seething with late-night static. As they watched, a lick of flame would yawn awake, swirling, growing, leaping into a sturdy column that would hold up the roof. As Jackson struggled, sweated, screamed, heat would creep over those curtains, trace the edges of the roof, consume everything around him while Jenna sat there, her skin like cool marble.

"Your fault," she would say.

As with every dream, the fire would surround the exit doors, pausing, almost as if testing Jackson, daring him to escape, to chase after it.

But no matter how much he fought, how much he raged, the fire always won, sprinting out the doors in a roar, a screech, a blaze of two children screaming in the night.

Even now, hours later, as Jackson steered Rip's rusted green pickup along the dusty road to town, a bead of panic drizzled down his temple. Merely thinking about that damned nightmare brought on the sweats again. His shirt was even soaked to his skin—and it wasn't in any part due to the Texas sun, either.

Next to him, Felicia started to fiddle with the air-conditioning instead of asking if he was okay. She probably knew he wouldn't give her a straight answer, so she was depending on action instead of words.

Smart, except nothing worked in the pickup besides the engine.

"We'll have to make do with the opened windows," he said, even though they weren't helping. The weather was sweltering today.

He couldn't get away from the heat.

"I appreciate your driving me," she reiterated.

Jackson nodded once, then took care to loosen his hold on the steering wheel. He was white-knuckling it.

She had to know that Jackson was driving her because Rip had asked. Otherwise, he was supremely discomfited on this shopping trip for Bobby.

But it wasn't his boss's fault. Jackson had never talked with the rancher about Leroy and Lucas, about his anguish at losing the children. It had been so damned unnatural; kids were supposed to outlast parents, tuck *them* into their deathbeds and cry tears of outrage.

Each day closer to Bobby's arrival brought the agony back in fresh waves. Jackson knew the fire dream had returned in full force because of Rip's nephew.

How was Jackson going to treat Bobby when he actually got here?

The question shook him to the core because he didn't know if he could handle himself day in and day out around another child.

Felicia seemed to sense his confusion and had been doing her best to put him at ease during this ride. Too bad she had no idea what was bothering him.

Too bad she kept tripping over the subject because he wouldn't tell her.

"I thought we'd start out in the Mercantile," she said. "They've got a big toy department."

"Then I'll head there."

The wind blew her hair against his arm and Jackson's eyes closed, just for the briefest second. The weight of contact stayed with him, buzzing his skin.

"You know," she said, sighing, "if you want to drop me off here, I can walk the rest of the way so you can get back to more important things."

Damn his taciturn nature. "I'm glad to drive you. Really."

If life had a laugh track, that would have been a cue for the audience to chime in.

Couldn't he drag himself out of these dumps? Even *he* was getting sick of the blues.

"Then I'll let you drive." Felicia crossed one skirted leg over the other, her ankle bobbing up and down.

On the vinyl seat next to him, she tapped her fingers.

Was she finding him tedious? That bruised. He wasn't a boring guy. Jeez, he used to be really carefree back when his hair didn't sport a touch of gray. At social functions, Jenna would always have to claim him by linking her arm through his and joke, "He's mine, girls. Don't you even think about it," just before he noticed that he'd been amusing a bunch of women with his laughter, his stories.

What had happened to *that* Jackson?

For the first time today, he gave Felecia a look that wasn't flummoxed, one that took all of her in: the flowing blue sundress, the smooth skin, the silver feather earrings that dangled from her ears. She'd pulled her platinum hair back in a ponytail, emphasizing a face that usually seemed to be thinking of a fun idea.

"That's a nice dress," he offered as a prelude to the new/old Jackson.

He *could* be the same guy, dammit.

She sat up a little straighter, ran a hand over her skirt. "Really?"

She angled her head, hinting that she had no idea where his compliment had come from.

"I suppose," he continued, "I should've found it within myself to spiff up, too, going to town and all."

"I was just in the mood. Sometimes that happens to women, you know. We like to wear pretty things to make us feel better." She touched an earring. "But you'd know that, I imagine."

If that was a cue to talk about women—like his ex-wife—as easily as she'd mentioned her ex-boyfriend yesterday, he wasn't up to the bait.

"Ah, well, wranglers don't know much about fancy dressing, I'm afraid."

See, talking was easy. Loosen the hardened bolts and let it flow. Even the tension in his shoulders was starting to ease up.

"Wranglers?" Felicia turned her body toward him, leaning an elbow on the back of the seat. "I've seen some cowboys put on the sparkle. Rhinestones, belt buckles…"

Jackson laughed.

"What?" she asked.

"Cowboys. You know they don't actually exist anymore? Figments of the American dream."

"Strange thing to say, especially coming from one."

"Me? I'm no cowboy. A wrangler? Sure. But the myth disappeared with the end of cattle drives and the introduction of cross-country trains."

As Jack relaxed his palm on top of the steering wheel, Felicia propped her head against her hand. Somehow, they'd fallen into a regular discussion, and she liked what it was doing to him.

His rugged face had grown a little more youthful, the squint lines around his eyes smoothing out. This close to him, she could take in his musky-leather scent and pretend he'd chosen to drive her to Wycliffe himself.

And that's what she did, just for a moment. Imagined.

"A lot of people who call themselves cowboys will be startled when they realize they're not what they think," she said.

"They can call themselves whatever they want while they two-step in their honky-tonks or ride their mechanical bulls. Wearing boots or knowing how to ride a horse doesn't make you a cowboy."

"Maybe I'm confused." She tugged on his shirtsleeve, hoping she wasn't overstepping her bounds in her quest for levity. "What *is* a cowboy?"

Donning a thoughtful expression, he didn't jerk away. See, *progress*. The whir of tires over cracked pavement and wind through the windows sounded reassuring now, soothing.

Finally, he lifted his chin a bit, narrowed his eyes. "Being a cowboy means having a sort of code, I guess. A nobility that went out of style. Someone who loves open spaces and the sound of grass blowing at night while he drinks coffee by the campfire. Someone whose heart is as wide as the ranges used to be and is too naive to realize that he can't be that way in a modern world." He paused. "A cowboy can stand and face anything that shows up to beat him down."

Felicia wanted to touch him again, to make sure he was real, to make sure she wasn't conjuring a guy who thought in simple poetry and believed in old-fashioned values.

In the end, Jack waved his commentary away, as if embarrassed to have spoken. "Show me someone like that, and you'll show me a real cowboy."

She wished she could tell him her definition, too: a man who had the power to give her everything she'd always yearned for.

As they pulled onto Wycliffe's Main Street, they passed those honky-tonks. Passed tourists from nearby dude ranches who were combing through Western boutiques and diners. Passed feedlots, supply stores, churches and a lone motel.

Jack's comments still filled her mind and, while parking at the curb in front of the Mercantile, Felicia couldn't help asking one more question.

"So there's no hope left for the myth, the cowboy?"

Because if there were no more, how would she find hers?

Jack cut the engine, stared straight ahead, a smile forming on his lips.

"Maybe there's one left."

Is it you, Jack North?

Before she could ask him to elaborate, he was out the door and around the cab to help her out.

As he took her hand, she tried to contain her giddiness, her pulse-pounding excitement. He grinned—that's right, yet another one—and tipped his hat as he let go and took a step away from her.

"You're not coming with me?" she asked.

Jack's grin disappeared and he looked into her eyes a beat too long, digging deep inside her for some reason.

Could he see that she was as anxious about Bobby as Rip was? That she was dying to make the boy feel at home?

Something seemed to pop in his gaze, not because he'd been broken. Because of a change. A snap in the wind. He seemed to be steeling himself against something.

Then resolutely, he placed his hand on the small of her back, guiding her toward the store.

Her heart beat double time.

"Okay, Felicia," he said. "Let's go inside."

Chapter Six

All too soon, the day came.

Stoverson had already set off with Rip to the airport so they could pick up Bobby, and at the Hanging R itself, the rest of the ranch hands were fixing themselves up for the express purpose of greeting the young boy.

Even Jackson had donned his best pair of jeans and a once-worn button-down. As he wandered out of the bunkhouse where Dutch and Carter were passing time by playing a round or two of poker, he caught sight of Felicia talking on the sunset-lit porch with Mrs. Krauss. She was the new housekeeper/cook Rip had brought on, a widowed family friend he'd managed to sweet-talk into helping him a few days ago.

A few days. It seemed more like a lifetime.

When Felicia had persuaded him to enter the Mercantile to buy Bobby toys, Jackson had taken his first step on a road that stretched into a different direction.

A road where every step frightened him because he'd been there before—and he knew what was probably waiting for him at the end.

Heartbreak? Soul-tearing regrets?

He'd feared both possibilities as they'd entered the store, Felicia smiling up at him every few minutes. It'd almost seemed as if she sensed his trepidation and had unconditionally offered encouragement.

In one of the toy aisles, she'd caught him off guard by firing up a green water gun and challenging him to a showdown like an old-school sheriff. Even though the old Jackson would've grabbed his own plastic weapon to engage in some fun nonsense, too, *this* Jackson wasn't quite there yet. Sure, he wanted to be, but stepping into this place for Rip's nephew was all he could manage today.

Still, he flashed a grin, and from the pleased look on Felicia's face, it was enough.

For now.

As they'd loaded toys and room furnishings into a cart, Jackson gained confidence, thinking that staying away from everything that reminded him of

Leroy and Lucas was actually far worse than confronting it.

But that was when they'd turned into the aisle with the miniature race cars.

He lost his ability to take in oxygen, visions of Lucas and his car collection blindsiding him.

All he could feel was Felicia's hand on his arm, her voice soothing him.

"Meet me outside?" she'd asked, obviously noticing his sudden change in willingness to be here.

Mutely, he'd nodded, then gone to the car to wait in the heat, bathing in sweat and memories—drowning, stifling, all-consuming.

Yet—woudn't you know it—when Felicia came back to him, she didn't prod for answers. And damned if he didn't feel a sight better as they drove away with her smiling over at him.

With her help, he'd taken the first step back toward a part of himself he'd been mourning. He couldn't avoid feeling that maybe, just maybe, Felicia Markowski might not mind walking with him on this new road inch by inch, day by day, backing him up in case he should fall.

Depending on her in this way mortified him. Still, since the shopping trip, he'd gained some serenity. There hadn't even been any fire dreams.

Until last night.

Jackson approached the porch, the orange-blue

tint of a day's end burnishing Felicia's unbound hair. She was favoring a different sundress today, one that reminded him of the first time he'd seen her, reminded him of pure prairies and wide skies. In contrast, Mrs. Krauss, the new housekeeper and cook, wore her gray hair in short, loose curls. Well-padded through the hips and stomach, she had a grandmotherly cast to her, smelling of gingerbread and wearing a long apron to cover a paisley housedress and knee-high panty hose. But her sensible shoes revealed her true nature: that of an iron-fisted kitchen goddess.

"Mr. North," Mrs. Krauss said, greeting him with a clipped nod and a heavy Germanic accent.

"Evening, ma'am." Then he smiled at Felicia. "Hi, there."

As always, she beamed at him, once again making him wonder what it was that always made her so happy to see him. Of course, he'd been spending more time with her since the Mercantile: helping her every night with the dishes, scooting closer and closer to her at the campfire until he was actually sitting a heart-thumping five feet away now.

Yeah, Felicia had invited him onto a different road, all right, but jeez, he hoped he wasn't going to be dependent on her in any way. That in itself presented a new problem, one he wasn't ready to face yet.

However, in the meantime, he'd enjoy her presence. After all, today was her last on the Hanging R since Mrs. Krauss was officially taking over cooking and cleaning duties. For the next few hours, at least, Jackson was somewhat relieved to know that Felicia would be around when Bobby got here.

Damn. Again with the growing dependency on her.

He could face Bobby on his own, couldn't he? He could be one of those cowboys he'd talked about— a man who stood up to his fears and problems. One of those ghosts of history he'd defined for Felicia as she'd sat next to him in the pickup, hanging on his every word.

Watching him with that beautiful tenderness in her gaze.

Felicia had turned to Mrs. Krauss, laying a hand on the older woman's arm.

"You need anything more from me?" she asked.

Was she leaving already? Before Bobby got here?

Jackson flinched, ashamed to want her around so badly.

Mrs. Krauss shook her head. "Believe it or not, Ms. Markowski, I have run a household before. Go." She waved her fingers toward the wild blue yonder. "I have dinner in hand."

"Great." On her way down the stairs, Felicia shot Jackson a mock-scared look, relaying her feelings about Mrs. Krauss.

She gestured toward the horse corrals and beyond. "Want to take a short walk before all the excitement breaks loose?"

"Sure." He tried to downplay his enthusiasm at the thought of being alone with her.

Heat dissipated in the still air, leaving the promise of a cooling twilight laced with the smell of hay, dust and animal. Their steps were fluid, matching each other. She was so close that he could almost feel the hum of her skin against his own.

"You look about ready to combust," she said, "and I needed a break from Empress Domestic. A walk seemed like the perfect solution."

He wasn't complaining. "She seems real strict, that Mrs. Krauss."

"A regular den mother. Thankfully, you'll only have to see her at mealtimes since she's taking over Rip's room and won't be around the bunkhouse to bark orders."

True enough. The living arrangements had been altered slightly this week: Rip would be staying in the bunkhouse permanently, allowing Mrs. Krauss to take night watch over Bobby. The boy would be living in the study, which had been converted into a pterodactyl-and-moon decorated boy's room.

The new cook had been lured here by Rip's guarantee of free rent, something Mrs. Krauss had snatched up right away. She'd been living with her daughter's family and hadn't been very happy about the lack of freedom. And with some money that came with Bobby, Rip could now afford the low salary Mrs. Krauss asked for.

It was a good, proper arrangement for everyone, Jackson thought. A spread of strays come together.

Unfortunately, Felicia was leaving, and that was a considerable drawback.

He laughed to himself, surprised to admit that he'd taken a shine to her. A shine that wouldn't ever come to anything, but a shine nonetheless.

"So," he said as they passed the corrals and headed toward the barn, "back to the grindstone for you."

"You mean Oakvale?"

They rounded the beaten gray planking of the barn's walls and she stopped, kicking at dirt with the toe of her shoe.

"It's not so much drudgery," she said. "I actually don't mind my job. Sure, there're parts of it that don't appeal, but…I don't know. I've got a good life there."

Felicia stared at the ground, picturing what she had going for her: friends, family, a tidy savings account that grew each month from the paychecks she didn't spend.

The Rhodeses provided housing for their servants—a real boon that kept the workers loyal and a part of the Oakvale community—so she didn't have to pay rent or spring for many meals. In fact, she'd spent more money this week than usual, quietly using her own credit card to buy Bobby the things Rip's cash hadn't covered. Items like the X-Wing Fighter models just waiting for the young boy to put together, or the Astros sheets that were waiting, crisp and clean, on his bed.

Jack had folded his lean frame against the barn wall, one leg bent to anchor him, a thumb hooked into his jeans pocket. In his other hand he held his hat, leaving his dark, silver-threaded hair ruffled, boyish. It didn't go at all with the sun-kissed skin or the crinkles around his eyes.

Merely glancing at him made her blood chug up and down her body.

So stoic. So mysterious.

He shot her a hesitant glance, then fixed his gaze on the horizon. "It'll sure be different without you around here."

"Different? In what way, exactly?"

He cleared his throat and started looking uncomfortable again.

Great. Just when she thought he'd taken a step forward, it always turned out to be a step back. But…

No, doggonit. She wasn't going to give up.

Maybe it was because night was falling and the sky was so hushed and gorgeous. Maybe it was because he seemed so lonely holding his hat in his hand. Or maybe it was because this was her last day on the Hanging R and she didn't know what sort of excuses she could invent to be around him again.

Whatever it was, she moved closer, slowly, almost as if he were a creature who would bolt if he saw her coming.

He did peek up from under those dark brows, but he didn't flinch. Didn't even glance away.

Progress.

She stopped, hardly daring to go farther.

A vein pulsed in his neck and her heart began to echo the rhythm.

"How's it going to be different around here, Jack?" she whispered.

His voice lowered, too. "I don't…" He thumped his hat against his thigh, tightened his jaw and swallowed. "Hell. I guess you brightened up the place. Kind of."

"That's…" Her smile made it hard to talk. "That's real nice."

He made a noncommittal sound, almost killing the moment. But she'd be darned if she let it die.

She took another step, blood slamming against her skin. It'd been an awfully long time since she'd found herself in this situation—dancing around expectation and when-will-he-make-a-move doubts. Nervous, terrible anticipation borne from previous experience.

Felicia knew what it was like to be with a man. Years ago, when she was much too young, she'd let one talk her into "going all the way." And it'd hurt, not just because she'd let down her family *and* her own morals, but physically, too. Later, she'd found out from a doctor that endometriosis could make intercourse painful, so she'd gone on some medication that *could* help if she wanted to try in the future.

However, the experience had been uncomfortable enough to make her gun-shy, persuading her to decide right there and then that the only man who'd ever make love to her again would be "the one."

With Jack, her body was telling her that he was it—not only the father of a someday child, but the man she'd be so in love with that she'd endure anything to be with him.

Gaining courage, she crept even nearer, a soft wind howling through the space between them.

"I think I'm going to miss you," she said.

Oh, God, please make it so that I haven't been misreading him the last few days. Please have it so that he's been thinking of kissing me, too.

His eyes got a tad wider, the irises bleeding into the dark centers, inviting her to solve the secrets they hid. He looked at her lips, caressing them with a gaze.

"I—" he finally glanced up into her eyes again "—guess I'll miss you, also."

Closer…

"Yeah?" she asked.

She slightly tilted her head, made Bambi eyes at him by glancing up. Holding her breath, she softly pressed her palms to his chest, feeling the bang of his heart pulsing into her.

"Yeah," he said, voice ragged.

His gaze went back to her lips, and she knew it was now or never.

Easing forward, she closed her eyes, brushed her mouth over his, breathing over him, reveling in the softness of the moist contact.

As she paused, savoring the moment, shock flowed through her, warmth skimming over her lips as he groaned, the sound barely discernable over the adrenaline pumping in her ears.

Was he going to avert his head and reject her? Push her away and retreat back into that cave of his?

As she kept her eyes shut and drew a mere whisper away from him, she readied herself for more of his apologies, for the end of her dream.

Her last cowboy, a myth. A lie she'd told herself so she could keep on hoping.

She licked her lips, still poised before him, then allowed her hands to slide down his chest in resignation. Just one touch before she admitted defeat.

She opened her eyes to find him staring at her, expression a blank.

"I'm sor—" she started to say.

His gaze expanded, exploding like a new world had been created inside him. With a burst of passion, he dropped his hat, surged forward, buried his hands in her hair and captured her mouth with his.

For a split second, she didn't process what was happening. Jack, dragging her against him, desperately kissing her as if she'd disappear if he didn't hold on tight enough.

But then it all flooded over her—his lips sucking at hers, his hands moving down, running over her back, searching upward, exploring her in a flare of undeniable heat.

Yes… Yes!

Ecstatic, she let herself fall against him, crashing them both back against the barn wall. Their breaths were choppy, cut off by more kisses, brands of moist affection stamping her neck, her face, her mouth.

"Felicia…." he said, almost as if in reverence.

He tasted of masculine spice: a tang of sweat on skin, a hint of mild soap and rawhide. She couldn't get enough of him, wanting to drink him in, own him, tell him about Carlota's prediction so he could see how right it was to be with her.

But even in the midst of this mindless desire, she knew that keeping mum about the last cowboy was a good idea. Jack needed to be persuaded, bit by bit. Knowing that he was her fate would probably scare him off.

Right? Of course she was right.

As he hitched her up, pulling her flush against the hard length of him—every growing, jeans-encased inch—she gave herself over, promising forever with her kisses.

That was when she heard the commotion. A horn blaring. Voices raised in welcome and laughter.

Jack must have caught it, too, because suddenly he was framing her face in his hands, his eyes unfocused, like a drunk man who'd overindulged.

Her pulse seemed to suspend itself, hovering, not knowing how to react.

"Jack?" she said, voice tiny, so unsure of itself.

His gaze cleared and for a second, she thought he was going to smile again, tell her everything would be all right now that their feelings were out in the open.

But she should have known better.

Instead, he stepped back from her, hands sliding down her arms until he'd grabbed her fingers.

"He's here," Jack said, sounding shell-shocked.

She wanted to believe that her adoration had dizzied him to this point, but she had a sneaking suspicion it wasn't true.

Why was it that every time the subject of Bobby came up, he got a haunted look about him?

"It's time to leave." He let go of her hands, then bent to pick up his hat.

Why was he acting like that kiss hadn't mattered? Was he sorry about doing it? Sorry that it'd ended?

What? *What?*

As he sent her an apologetic glance, Felicia told herself not to take it to heart. Nope. Instead, she'd keep smiling. Stay optimistic.

That's right, she thought as he started to walk away, keeping his pace slow so she'd catch up, she supposed.

Even if he'd just ended things, Jackson North had kissed her right back when she'd invited him to.

And that was a sure sign from destiny if there ever was one.

He was still burning up from that kiss, even two hours later as they all sat at the outside table eating dinner.

In fact, Jackson thought, using a slab of bread to stir Mrs. Krauss's beef stew in its bowl, he could still catch the scent of Felicia on him. It lightened him up, somehow, even if he had every reason to be in the gray.

Speaking of which... He took a gander at six-year-old Bobby, the new kid on the block.

Dark brown curls in need of a good cut. Blue eyes. A pug nose and chubby cheeks. The child hadn't smiled yet, but from careful yet discreet observation, Jackson knew he was missing one upper tooth near the right side of his mouth.

That got to Jackson. Neither Leroy nor Lucas had grown old enough to lose their baby fat, much less their teeth.

Poor boy. Everyone was going full steam ahead, trying to engage the kid in conversation, attempting to make him feel welcome at a table of adults who were getting more concerned by the second.

Just look at him sitting there, he thought. All shrugged up into himself, watching his bowl of stew as if it would suck him in and take him back to a mother and father who'd died young—victims of a helicopter accident while on a second honeymoon in Maui.

Jackson could imagine Bobby's shock, how it would last a long time, become something like a hard, second skin.

Across the table, Felicia finally stopped serving everyone—much to Mrs. Krauss's territorial pleasure—sat down and watched Jackson watch Bobby.

He was telegraphing too much information with all this perusing, wasn't he?

Jackson went back to playing with his food, trying not to dwell on outside stimuli that had wormed way too far inside him.

Kisses, petal-soft skin under his fingertips, lust flaming his brain to a crisp.

"Bobby?" he heard her ask. "Would you like more stew? Or are you ready for some dessert?"

Jackson glanced up at the boy. He must be a masochist, visually touching base with this child every minute, almost as if he couldn't get his fill of the youth, the lost opportunities of his own sons.

Even the mention of sweets didn't get to Bobby. He only kept staring at his food.

"How about ice cream?" she asked, leaning her elbows on the table and lowering herself so she could catch the boy's eye. "We've got an old-fashioned maker that your uncle Rip pulled out of storage just for you."

Bobby shot a quick peek at her.

"You can even be in charge of turning the crank," Felicia continued. "It's really an important job. Not everyone can do it, especially me. I'm awful at working that crank. You have to be mechanically inclined—like someone who can build or fly spaceships."

At the mention of his hobby, Bobby sat straighter, suddenly interested.

It was easier for the child to think about spaceships than his parents, Jackson imagined.

"So," Felicia added, "can you be in charge of that? Cranking? I'd be grateful because I love ice cream. We can have a lot of it after we both finish dinner. All right?"

Bobby offered a silent nod.

Yes! Yeah. Well… Good.

Just why the hell was Jackson celebrating? Was it because of the pleased grin Felicia wore as she grabbed her water glass? Or was it because Bobby had picked up his spoon to fill it with stew and take a bite?

Much to Jackson's astonishment, she proceeded to draw Bobby out, causing him to look up from his food for more than ten seconds at a time.

"What kind of spaceship would you want to fly?" she asked.

Bobby thought about it. "A rocket ship." Okay, so the boy was mumbling, but it was a positive sign.

"Ah." There was a lilt in Felicia's voice as she conversed with him, but she never talked down to Bobby. Never pretended she was above his interests. "Nice choice. Good old-fashioned rockets are like hot rods compared to the space shuttle, huh?"

He nodded his head.

"Rockets have some character, all right." She made a half-goofy face that made Bobby smile. "When I was younger, I used to imagine the first astronauts circling the moon and trying to lasso them from those rockets."

"Like cowboys?"

"Exactly." Felicia cut a fresh piece of bread for the boy and handed it to him. He accepted without question as her gaze snagged Jackson's. "Just like cowboys."

Bobby dipped his bread in the stew, bit into it and ate while he talked more and more about a galaxy far, far away. His voice had even improved from its initial muttering. Even though Felicia had to kiddingly remind him to chew slower, he was responding to her, warming up to at least one of the Hanging R bunch.

From the near-silence at the table, Jackson knew that everyone else was noticing, also. Especially Rip, whose eyes held a mixture of contentment and heartache.

No doubt the old rancher was wondering if he would be able to connect with Bobby as Felicia had. But, judging from Rip's past performances, Jackson knew he would succeed.

Rip had more perseverance than anyone.

Later, as Bobby took control of the ice-cream maker, Jackson took pride in how his boss made a heroic effort to befriend his great-nephew.

Weighed down with all his troubles, Rip still had the heart to put Bobby first.

"Hurray," Felicia said, coming to stand next to Jackson in front of the campfire. "A good start."

He tried to make believe he hadn't kissed her only hours ago, hadn't mapped the curves of her back with his hands, hadn't wanted to take her in his arms and lay her in the grass where her hair would spread out like a setting sun.

"Bobby's still going to be living in a world of

hurt," Jackson said. "It'll be a while before he learns to cope without his parents."

She was quiet for a moment, deep in thought. Jackson knew she was connecting some of his dots, piecing together the words he left out of conversations.

Meanwhile, Mrs. Krauss brought Bobby and Rip some ice-cream bowls. The two adults exchanged a few barbs before the new cook went on her way.

A little sexual tension between old friends? Jackson thought.

But when Rip went right back to helping Bobby without another glance at "Empress Domestic," Jackson dismissed the speculation.

Maybe his own head was too caught up in clouds of lust and it was coloring everything around him.

"Well." Felicia nodded, turned to face him. "I suppose it's time for me to leave."

A heaviness fell over him. "But…ice cream. Aren't you staying for dessert?"

"Maybe a scoop. I've got to go but I wanted to talk to you alone before I do."

Panic rushed him. Dammit, that kiss had given her ideas he hadn't been in favor of encouraging.

"Felicia…"

Mrs. Krauss interrupted by taking Felicia's hand and pulling her toward the ice-cream maker.

"Hurry, scoop it up before it melts," she said.

Felicia tried to resist. "But—"

She was dragged away by the bigger woman, casting a helpless glance back at Jackson. He took a moment to thank Mrs. Krauss and her bossiness.

There would be no more kisses for him. No more of this madness or the growing need to rely on Felicia's bright nature.

Bobby's presence would be a thorn in his side, but he would overcome the agony, keep traveling that new road he'd chosen because the little boy needed a problem-free environment right now—not a wrangler with an allergy to children.

As the distance grew between him and the woman he'd held in his arms today, Jackson breathed easier.

Even if he suspected his nightmares would burn him alive tonight.

Chapter Seven

"She returns in victory," Carlota said.

It was the morning after Felicia had come back from the Hanging R, and she was just now getting ready to report back to Oakvale housekeeping duty. Carlota was leaning against her friend's cottage wall after shutting the door and handing Felicia her mail. ABBA played on the boom box, as usual, and, as the blonde cha-cha-cha-ed to "Fernando," she gestured for her fellow maid to sit on a beanbag.

The feisty housekeeper, dressed like Felicia in Oakvale's black-and-white maid uniform, quirked her eyebrow and remained standing. After Emmy had married Deston, she'd left Carlota and Felicia to flip a coin over who would get to live in this quaint shelter in lieu of the mansion's downstairs quarters, where most of the household staff dwelled.

And guess who'd come out on top? Yes, the same person who'd kissed Jack North yesterday.

In the meantime, Carlota was still doing her best to get over the fact that she'd lost the coin toss for the cottage, acting like she was a guest, probably just to get Felicia's goat. Her friend was convinced the adorable quarters were meant to be hers. She hadn't gotten a vision about it—she was just that stubborn. That was one reason she wouldn't sit down and relax; the other had more to do with antsiness.

"Are you going to tell me about that big, dopey smile on your face or what?" Carlota asked.

Felicia sat on her bed and sorted through her mail with verve. "Things are great. Rip's nephew is somewhat settled in, and I think he's latched on to me. He asked me last night whether I'd be around the ranch anymore."

"And, naturally, you will be."

Yes, thought Felicia. Not that she would use Bobby as an excuse to see Jack again, but life was making it pretty easy to do so. Truth was, Felicia had taken a great liking to Bobby and would have come back to the Hanging R to see him anyway.

But that happened with a lot of children, even though they all didn't train big, sad blue eyes on her.

"Oh, yeah," Felicia added, as if in afterthought, "and I kissed Jack."

Carlota gave an excited hop away from the wall. "I knew it! Was it…I don't know. Worthy of the planets aligning?"

"Uh-huh." Felicia sighed. "Very much so."

While Carlota took up where Felicia had left off dancing to "Fernando"—one, two, cha-cha-cha— Felicia laughed and concentrated on the mail. And Jack. And that kiss.

The roughness of a five-o'clock shadow against her cheeks, the tempo of his quickened breathing…

Another sigh, then back to reality.

It was relatively boring, as far as mail went. There was nothing but catalogs she wouldn't order from anyway. She wasn't a big splurger, except when it had come to Bobby, she guessed. Sure, she was thrifty with the decent wages she earned but, unlike Emmy and Carlota, Felicia hadn't fully embraced the same "poor complex" they'd all grown up with. In spite of the way Felicia, too, had wished to have nice dresses and pretty ponies like the wealthy guests who frequently visited Oakvale, she had never resented the Rhodes family for their riches or obsessed about what it would be like to have whatever she wanted.

Except when it came to family, of course. And being a woman.

Back in grade school, when she, Emmy and Carlota had attended those first life-altering sex-education classes, the teachers had talked about female reproductive systems and having babies. Felicia had gone home, unpacked all her old dolls and held them while a faraway longing took shape in her chest. She'd chattered nonstop to her now-long-deceased mother about the day she would marry a man who loved her and how they would make sons and daughters—just like all her relatives.

Her mom had hugged her, filling Felicia with joy, making her feel as if she belonged.

Years later, after that heartbreaking "woman's trip" to the doctor, her dreams had smashed into a million shards.

Adoption is a good alternative, doctor after doctor had said. *We can put you on medication, but even though it might help you with the pain you feel with intercourse and your period, it isn't a cure. We can try surgery, but even that's no guarantee.*

Damaged.

A hollowness seized her. Why had she been given the capacity to love so openly and deeply when she would probably never be rewarded with her own child?

As ABBA and Carlota charged on, Felicia took a

cleansing breath, shoving aside the threatening bitterness. Instead, she resumed her mail search, stopping cold when she came to a local newsletter
announcing a rodeo that was coming to town.

Toby, the ex, was a featured bull rider.

Carlota danced to Felicia's side, read the text,
stopped. "He's coming here to compete?"

"You've got it."

Toby Baker. A good old boy with good old
dreams. He'd wanted a big family with little rustlers
who looked just like him, shaggy hair and all. She'd
been very fond of Toby but, in hindsight, hadn't
been in love. Sure, she'd hoped every night that it
would turn into something more, but it hadn't. Even
so, he'd had the power to crush her feelings with one
horrified reaction.

A meal of sirloin, rosemary-laced green beans
and fancy potatoes served amid candlelight and
Beethoven. A confession from Toby—who'd slicked
down his hair and had been wearing a tie even
though Felicia had known it had to be choking him.
A spark of optimism lighting her hopes after he'd
told her he wanted to be with her for the rest of his
life.

Until *her* confession.

The slow-dawning realization, pulling his lips
into a half grimace.

We could adopt if surgery didn't work, she'd said,

grabbing at straws, knowing what his look meant because she'd seen it before with other boyfriends who'd gotten serious. Gradually, she'd learned to keep the matter to herself, until Toby and his "let's be together forever" talk had come around.

Silently, they'd continued dinner and, later that night, he'd made the phone call to her.

Heck, Toby wasn't her future anyway. Sure, he'd been the "last cowboy" she'd dated, but Jack North had to be *the one* instead.

Yet what if Jack reacted the same way? Would he ever want to kiss her again if he knew she didn't have much chance of being whole?

Felicia refolded the newsletter and calmly put it on the bed. She still didn't have the guts to tell Carlota about how Toby had treated her or even about how Jack might react. Voicing her fears would only make her feel worse.

Instead, she kept it all inside, putting on a sunny face.

She realized Carlota had been taking stock of her with a worried gaze.

Time for a change of subject. *Pronto.*

"Do you think Fritz still collects comic books?" she asked Carlota, referring to one of the kitchen workers.

"Are you kidding?" Concern lingered in Carlota's dark eyes, but she knew better than to say anything once Felicia had made up her mind not to talk about it. "Fritz without his comics is like M&M's without the colorful candy coating. Why?"

Bobby, that's why. "I know a little boy who'd love to check out any decent books Fritz might want to spare."

"Then let's catch him before we start work."

Thank goodness Carlota wasn't asking more questions, because Felicia was in no mood to address them.

Not when she didn't have any answers.

As the sun fell, painting the hilly landscape with brushstrokes of rust, gold and lavender, Felicia pulled into the Hanging R, her passenger seat filled with a box of non-vintage comics Fritz had given her. He'd had some hardbound "funnies" titles, like *Captain Underpants* and *Scooby-Doo*, books Fritz hadn't cared too much about beyond one-time reads. Felicia had forked over thirty dollars to him, thinking it was a deal to procure these light, entertaining stories—no angst-ridden superheroes or end-of-the-world scenarios for Bobby.

She'd arrived just after dinner, in time to catch the hands settling around their campfire, Mrs. Krauss scurrying into the cabin with the dishes and J-Wayne trotting around to the back of the cabin in pursuit of a furry creature.

When Felicia got out of her Pontiac, Bobby was there to meet her as if he'd been rooted to this spot in the ground all along, waiting patiently.

Like yesterday, he was still much too serious for a kid, no smiles, no mischievous gleam in his eyes. Just a Spider-Man T-shirt, jeans and tennis shoes.

"Hi," she said, taking the comics box out of the car. "Did you have fun today?"

She knew he wouldn't be starting school until the fall and that gave him all kinds of time to waste on the ranch during the day. Rip had foregone his work duties to be with Bobby, and although Felicia admired him for it, she knew there was now one less worker to get the Hanging R back in fighting shape.

"Uncle Rip put me on a horse for the first time," Bobby said.

Felicia couldn't tell whether he'd liked that or not. "Did you fall off?" she joked.

He made a "phhfft" sound, shuffling his feet. "Of course I didn't. Uncle Rip made me put on a hat and I rode old Candy Cane around and around."

She knew Bobby probably meant *safety helmet* instead of *hat.* She started to walk toward the other adults, who were shouting out hearty welcomes. Waving at them the best she could with a box in her hands, she headed toward the lit porch, where she deposited her load.

Jack wasn't with the others, and disappointment

cloaked her, making the fading colors of the approaching night a little dimmer.

Curiously, the small boy pointed at her box. "What's that?"

Felicia peeked inside, snapped the lid back down. "Something that doesn't breathe or bark, but I think you'll like them all the same."

Bobby moved closer to her, sat on the porch steps and stared at the box as if that would make it open by itself.

Laughing, Felicia couldn't stand to tease anymore. "Dig in. See how you like them."

No time was wasted on Bobby's part. With Christmas-morning pep, he flung off the lid, then got to his knees to peer inside.

"Whoa," he said, reaching in and extracting an issue of *Pokemon*. "This is neat."

She wondered how much he would be able to read, but knew he would be amused with the pictures. "I was betting you'd like these. Creative people usually do."

"Thanks." Immediately, Bobby flopped to his butt, burying himself in the vivid panels and dialogue bubbles.

He moved his mouth while trying to read, and warmth suffused her. Casually, she ruffled his hair, disturbing his curls. Bobby didn't seem to mind— or maybe he was just too smitten with his presents to care.

When she finally glanced away from him, she realized they weren't alone.

Jack was loitering near the side edge of the porch, under a slant of shadow. She hadn't seen him there previously, seated on the ground with his legs drawn up, resting his forearms on his thighs while he whittled.

Under the brim of his hat, he was watching her and Bobby, his knife frozen over the wood, as if he'd been in the middle of a cut and hadn't ever finished.

From the looks of it, he was in his own world, thinking his own random Jack North thoughts.

He'd been the same way last night, keeping his distance from Bobby, even though they'd been sitting right next to each other at the dinner table.

Didn't he like children?

Uh-oh.

Felicia chanced a tiny wave at him, wondering if he was even aware she existed.

After a pause, he shook himself out of whatever reverie he was in, nodded back to her.

Went back to whittling.

Snick. Snick....

It was as if they didn't even know each other.

Her heart dropped to her stomach, flopping around, making her a little ill.

What was with him?

Snick. Snick....

Silence.

He'd come to rest his forearms on his knees now. Huddled over, one hand pushed back his hat so that it exposed the rest of his face. A frown rested on his mouth. He shook his head, then glanced at her.

Well, darn it, if the mountain wouldn't come to Felicia, Felicia would go to the mountain.

With a pat on Bobby's leg, she climbed down to the ground, reassuring herself that the child was so caught up in his funnies that he didn't even know she was gone. In a few more steps, she was in front of Jack, standing over him, still in sight of Bobby.

"Felicia," Jack said by way of greeting.

He said it softly, gently. His low voice caressed her name, sending shivers over her skin, in spite of the night's warmth.

"Jack." She rested her hands on her hips. "What're you doing over here in purgatory?"

His eyebrows raised, and the word earned a melancholy smile. "Purgatory. Not far from the mark."

What was he talking about? And what was going on with his mood? She was all for a brooding cowboy, but not after what had happened between them yesterday. Jack was supposed to be the real thing—not some cooked-up fantasy.

Or…yeesh. Maybe she *was* wasting her time with him, throwing coins into a wishing well that had been dry for years.

"Well, then," she said, "have a good sulk, Jack."

She started to go back to Bobby, who'd stopped his comics-gazing long enough to smile at her.

Aw.

"Wait…Felicia." Jack sounded exasperated—not with her, though. With himself. "I'm…just getting used to things around here lately. And I can't say the overall tone of the Hanging R is sky high tonight."

"Why?"

Jack folded the knife back into itself. "I finally talked Rip into selling some land. Six hundred acres, in fact. He's inside right now, looking over the books, thinking up every excuse to hold on to his property. It's been in the family for generations, so I can't blame him for being stubborn. 'No McCain has ever sold out,' he keeps telling me."

"Oh, jeez, Rip." Why did the worst things happen to the best people? "I'm sorry to hear that."

The thunk, thunk of footsteps on wood told her that Bobby was coming down the steps. Looking over, she saw that he had a comic book in hand, the pages flapping by his side.

As soon as the boy came to Felicia, Jack stiffened up.

Did his reluctance to mingle have something to do with Bobby, as well as the ranch? Did Jack blame the child for further ruining Rip's circumstances? After all, it hadn't escaped her attention that he thought the world of the old man and would defend him against anything.

"See?" Bobby said to Felicia, pointing to a picture of Captain Underpants battling some kind of booger monster.

"Pretty nasty there," Felicia said, more out of life-disgust than snot abhorrence, because after hearing Rip's news, she wasn't really all that chipper anymore.

At the same time, she couldn't help noticing that the boy kept shooting Jack interested looks, much like he'd been doing with her last night—testing, seeking. Deciding whom he could trust.

Was Bobby as wary of Jack as the wrangler was of the child?

Great. More tension on the Hanging R.

Something protective within her stirred. She laid her hand on Bobby's shoulder, lightly, merely for a moment. Enough to tell him she'd always be there.

The little boy went back to his comics, although he did stay by her side. It was enough for her.

Since dwelling on Rip's economic plight was out of the question with Bobby here, she thought some small talk might be in order, a breezy conversation letting the boy know that everything was neat and tidy at his new home, that he wasn't a burden to anyone.

That he was a part of the family now.

"Speaking of slimy stuff, how was Mrs. Krauss's latest meal?" she asked Jack.

The wrangler visibly relaxed. "It wasn't lasagna, but I can live with sauerkraut and sausage, I suppose. It fills the stomach nicely."

"I want Mrs. Krauss to make spinach," Bobby noted, glancing up from his book. "Just like Popeye eats."

Jackson tried not to think about how his sons used to watch the sailor-man reruns on TV every Sunday morning. How he himself used to hunker down in front of the screen with them, Leroy cuddled in his lap as Lucas leaned against his arm. They'd laugh at the foiled antics of Popeye's archenemy, Bluto, together, then try to convince Jenna to serve spinach for dinner.

It'd been the best way to make them eat vegetables, he thought, his heart cracking.

He kept his gaze on the folded knife, the formless piece of wood he'd been attacking earlier. Anywhere but on Bobby.

"I prefer broccoli, myself," Felicia said to the child. "Covered in hollandaise sauce…mmm."

"What's holiday sauce?" Bobby asked, nose shriveled.

Jackson couldn't help himself. "It's something that hides the awful taste of broccoli."

Bobby's eyes widened, probably because the last thing he'd expected was to see Jackson addressing him. Ever.

Even Felicia seemed flabbergasted. Pleased, but flabbergasted.

Hell, he had it in him to relate to kids, too.

But…what was he thinking? Had he been goaded by the easy way Felicia related to Bobby? Was he envious in some warped way?

Yup. Real jealous, as a matter of fact. He kind of wanted to be liked by Bobby, he supposed. The sentiment was mixed up with admiration for Felicia and a gut-warming realization that this woman would make a damned fine mother someday.

When she found the right man to have children with.

Jackson tried to swallow past the tight dryness in his throat. The right man. A *good* man.

The best, because that's what she deserved.

"Do you like broccoli?" Bobby ventured to ask Jackson. His voice was soft, cautious.

Felicia was fighting a smile. "I'm going to check in with Rip and I'll be right back, okay?"

She took off, and even though Jackson knew she was only going inside the cabin to fawn over Rip and make him feel better, he wanted to yell at her to come back. She'd deserted him, left him alone with his very own version of wolf bane.

Bobby was waiting for him to respond to his broccoli question, looking as serious as ever.

Jackson didn't have a mean enough bone in his

body to refuse the boy. He would live through this stilted interaction.

"I despise any kind of food that sprouts from the ground." There. Good enough?

His hands were aching to busy themselves, but he didn't want to flash his knife with Bobby standing right here. That was part of the reason he'd chosen to whittle privately in the first place.

"Sometimes bad food makes you strong though," the boy said. "That's what my mom told me."

Suddenly the crickets seemed too loud. The hoot of an owl screeched instead of lulled. A sheen of moisture dulled Bobby's gaze and his bottom lip trembled.

What a tough guy, Jackson thought. Bobby was trying to hold it all in.

His mom. Parents. Dead. Plucked out of this little boy's life by some vicious twist of fate.

Jackson knew exactly how Bobby was feeling. "Did you know," he said, trying to lift the boy's suddenly dampened spirits, "that sugar can be healthy, taken in small doses, of course?"

Bobby's shake of the head was almost violent. A tear rolled down his face.

"Oh. Hey, now."

Jackson didn't know what to do. The idea of patting the boy on the shoulder as he'd seen Felicia do sent terror scurrying down his spine. But, dammit, he couldn't leave Bobby like this.

Drawing on all his strength, Jackson reached out, took the boy's wrist. He still had a layer of baby fat and the feel of it stabbed Jackson right in his chest.

"Crying's all right," Jackson added, barely getting the words past the pain swollen in his throat.

And Bobby did cry, soundlessly, cheeks reddened with his tears.

Aw, damn. Jackson made a defeated sound, then reluctantly drew Bobby into something resembling a hug. It was desperate, stiff, too tight—almost as if he were holding on to something he'd just lose again—but it was the *right* thing to do. Something that would bring a shine to Felicia's eyes.

As he suffered through the boy's anguish with Bobby slumping against him, the toughened wrangler patted the boy's back and looked up at the star-pocked sky, vowing not to break down himself.

Somewhere up there, his boys and Bobby's parents were together, wishing their loved ones wouldn't be so sad.

He pictured Leroy and Lucas, just as proud as Felicia would be to see him sacrificing his protective fear for this little boy who needed some comfort.

That's good, Daddy, the kids would've said. *We needed someone to hold us, too, after we left you.*

Suddenly, Jackson realized how important his next reaction would be to Bobby—how damned much he wanted the child to feel as safe as he would've wanted his sons to be for the rest of their lives.

When Bobby calmed down, Jackson lowered his voice. "Want to know a secret?"

The boy pulled back, keeping hold of Jackson's hands, hitching in his breath with three quick gasps, seemingly glad to concentrate on another subject.

"I lost people I loved, too, so I know what you're going through. And any time you want to tell me how awful it is, you do that. Got it, Bobby?"

He sniffed, rubbed at his eye with the hand that was still holding the comic. With the other, he twisted Jackson's fingers in his own. "I got it."

"All right, then."

The little boy pulled himself together, then asked, "Who are *your* dead people?"

Jackson bit the inside of his lip so hard that he tasted blood.

The fluid filled his mouth with a taste of bitter metal, as if he were biting down on something that was holding back a scream. Finally, he let go of Bobby's hand.

"My sons," he choked out.

Bobby apparently empathized because he bent down and patted Jackson on *his* shoulder.

"Don't worry," he whispered. "It's our secret."

Then, unaware of how much he'd just ripped

Jackson down the middle, Bobby plunked down next to him and proceeded to read his book.

Soon, Felicia returned, finding Bobby peaceful and Jackson still mired in his own heavy emotions. She herself had shadows in her gaze, and all Jackson wanted to do was erase them with more kisses.

Wanted to take her into his arms and steady his imbalance with the feel of her.

Instead, he merely kept his secret.

Even though he didn't know how much longer he wanted to hide it from her.

Chapter Eight

Days later in Wycliffe, a weekend crowd filled the old Western streets, buying souvenirs and chambray shirts, hats and hand-tooled leather belts.

Felicia herself was tending to her own business.

Crocheting magazines, she thought, walking out of a crafts shop. Felicia had been so busy with Bobby, the Hanging R and her last cowboy that she hadn't been keeping up with her newest hobby—something that kept her anxious hands busy and served to relax her.

Doilies and delicate sweaters. Felicia sighed. They still wouldn't take her mind off what Rip was enduring. While visiting Bobby these last few nights—spending time with the child had become a habit as ingrained as eating dinner or saying a bedtime prayer—she'd noticed smudges etching their way under the elderly rancher's eyes.

Though he pretended to be as lively as a new pup around her, she knew he was struggling more than ever. The realization concerned her enough to literally beg Rip to accept monetary help from his neighbors, but he always made light of her suggestions, repeating over and over, "Come hell or high water, McCains will always float to the top."

As Felicia sauntered down Main Street to her car, parked near Woodrow's, a bustling bar that the locals favored, she thought that, at the very least, Bobby was doing well. Sure, he would wipe away silent tears every so often and Felicia would do her darnedest to comfort him, but he was adjusting as well as could be expected to life on the ranch.

Life without his parents.

Yet, like a true family, even Dutch, Carter and Stoverson had banded together to welcome the child, encouraging Bobby to sit by the campfire at night while Carter attempted to relay his questionable expertise on the harmonica. And Mrs. Krauss, bless her efficient heart, was hovering over him as a grandmother would, stuffing him with treats of strudel and baked apples, homemade jams and marzipan.

Felicia was confident that things would even out at the Hanging R. They had to. If anyone could right the ranch's troubles, it would be Rip McCain, who'd inherited the land from a long line of other McCains dating back to his horse-stealing great-great-granddad.

Having come to her car, Felicia opened the passenger's side and slid her magazines onto the seat. As she was closing the door, a familiar voice greeted her.

"You find the most pleasant views through a bar window."

It was Stoverson, pushing open one of the bar's swinging doors. He cuffed back his hat so it showed his leathered face, his scholar's brow. Twangy music from Hank Williams Jr. backed up the ranch hand as he grinned at her.

"Hey, there," she said.

After Felicia closed her car door and wandered closer, she glanced at the bar's stark, hazy front window. Through the thick glass, she could detect a high empty table, two deserted longnecks on either side. Though he'd obviously enjoyed company, Stoverson must have spotted her and come straightaway to the door.

"Hope I didn't interrupt anything," she said, ready to tease him about hiding a girlfriend in town.

But then Jack pushed open the other side of the swinging doors, nudging up his own hat in greeting.

Chancing a smile at her, he said, "Afternoon, Felicia."

Her stomach did a thrill-ride flip-flop. Smiling. Jack. An oxymoron if there ever was one.

"Hi," she said, testing him, wondering how long that smile would last.

When it proved to have staying power, her insides did one more extra spin, just to make sure she was marking this moment, Felicia guessed.

She had no idea why her body hadn't gotten used to him by now. It was true she hadn't seen him for a day or two—he wasn't always around when she visited Bobby, and really, she'd begun to wonder if he was purposely avoiding her for some reason—so maybe she was just having to start from square one again?

Doggonit, she would probably have to build up some kind of Jack-immunity bit by bit so, one day, she wouldn't feel as goofy around him.

At any rate, she couldn't hold back her own smile. She never could.

"And what are you two troublemakers doing at Woodrow's on a Saturday afternoon?" she asked.

"Looking at pretty girls through the window," Stoverson said.

Jack shot him the stink eye, as if warning his fellow wrangler away from Felicia. A carnal jolt caught her by surprise, surging just below her belly in a place that hadn't been affected for a really long time.

For a second, she could almost buy into the fantasy that she was his woman. *All* woman.

Jack took a step forward, positioning himself inches ahead of Stoverson while putting his weight against the rough pine door frame. A territorial statement?

"Rip gave us a few hours off," he said, "so we're here making the most of it."

Again, she peeked at the grubby window, the two beers.

"But," Jack said quickly, "we just got started with our relaxing. First drinks of the day, as a matter of fact, and there won't be much more afterward."

"Is that the truth?" Stoverson shot his comrade a curious glance. "I lost the designated-driver coin toss so you could have one beer?"

A laugh bubbled out of Felicia, capturing their attention. Both men stood up straighter, grinning at her.

So many smiles. Was this her regular Jack or had someone replaced him with a newer model?

Or maybe that wasn't it at all. Maybe he was… Oh, she could barely think it….

Maybe he was actually coming around?

She stopped herself from giving a tiny squeal of excitement. "Glad you two are having a good time,"

she said instead, so much more demurely than that
nearly escaped *whee!*

"Want to join us?" Jack asked, the words rushed.
For a second, he reminded Felicia of a young man
who'd made his way across a dance floor and sucked
up enough courage to lure her away from the wall
with an invitation to spend a song in his arms.

At her pause, his face reddened and he immediately seemed to brace himself for a no.

"I have a better idea." Stoverson gave Jack a poke
toward the street. "I'll talk to that redhead who
winked at me from her bar stool and you'll grab
some fresh air."

With that, the smooth-talking ranch hand disappeared into the festive darkness of Woodrow's, the
half door swinging in his absence.

Leaving Jack to stand with Felicia.

A beat passed before he gestured in the general
direction of Wycliffe itself. "You on your way
home?"

"I was, but…" She allowed the subtle hint for him
to get his rear end out here to linger.

"Well…" He cast one last glance inside Woodrow's, shrugged, stepped onto the planked sidewalk.
"Want to take a turn around the area?"

It was the first time he'd made the initial move.
True, Stoverson had just about planted his boot in
Jack's jeans to get him outside, but here he was.

"I'd like that," she said, flashing a smile.

He ambled outside. One step for Jack, one giant leap for progress.

His boot heels echoed with every footfall. Once or twice, his checkered cotton shirt brushed against her bare arm and goose bumps sprang to life over her skin.

This felt nice, just walking with him. No need for forced conversation, right?

So then why were the words screaming to get out? Was she starting to feel nervous because *he'd* taken control this time?

The turnabout jittered her pulse, gave this jaunt an air of expectant mystery.

Soon, they'd left the shops behind, and an expanse of green grass and playground noises awaited them. Wycliffe Park, with its artistic yet functional amusements. There was a sombrero-shaped merry-go-round, a wheelbarrow-inspired slide, swings hanging from the arches of an upright cement rattlesnake and a Davy Crockett statue in the midst of a spraying fountain. Children and their parents laughed with each other in the sandbox, on the monkey bars. A little girl in pigtails chased two panting Maltese dogs around an ice-cream cart.

Felicia broke the quiet between her and Jack, unable to hold back any longer. "This would be a great place to bring Bobby. Maybe I could do that on one of my days off."

"I'm sure wherever you take him, he'd like it just fine."

As a young boy with spiked hair and glasses ran past them, Felicia couldn't help noticing that Jack's gaze was suddenly troubled. Out of sorts.

All too familiar around children.

"Can I ask you something?" she said. "It's nothing you have to answer, though."

With a touch to her elbow, he nodded, guided her toward a copse of oak trees, their leaves providing cool shade over quiet trails winding into more privacy.

"Ask away," he said.

"All right." The crystalline hustle of a stream welcomed them into the woods. "I've noticed you seem kind of removed with Bobby. You've gotten somewhat more comfortable since the day he showed up, but there's still a distance about you."

He didn't say anything for a moment. Then, tentatively, he spoke.

"I suppose I need warming up when it comes to people in general."

No kidding.

They came to a tiny, sun-dappled wooden bridge that spanned the creek. Brown paint flaked off it and several boards had splintered away to reveal the sparkling water rushing by underneath.

Felicia rested her hand on a rail. In a small way,

it steadied her. "You took long enough to trust me to be alone with you. Remember that first day at the charity fair? You were like a scared rabbit, ready to bolt every time I made a comment."

There was that smile again, thank goodness. Hard to come by, but so worth the effort.

"I remember," he said.

"So that's what's going on with Bobby?" she said, determined to get to the bottom of his cryptic behavior. "You're just warming up to him?"

His features became a battleground: emotion warred in his dark eyes, the lines around his mouth. He swallowed hard, then hitched his thumbs into his jeans pockets.

"I've been working up to telling you a few things," he said. "Not because they need telling, exactly, but because… Aw, hell. Sometimes a man needs to unburden himself."

"Yes, he does."

Still, Jack didn't pursue the matter. He merely continued his personal fight as he stared at the dried leaves littering the dirt.

All she could hear was the stream gushing over the rocks, the cry of a bird high up in the trees. She wasn't going to force him to tell her a thing. God, she wanted to hear him talk so badly, but if she'd learned anything, it was that Jack got ready on his own schedule.

Pushing him didn't seem right.

"Bobby reminds me of someone," he finally said, voice thick. "Two someones, actually."

His words skidded to a halt and he held up a finger.

Felicia moved away from the bridge, tentatively reaching out to lay a hand on his opposite arm. Under her fingers, his muscles bunched.

"Who?" she said, overwhelmed by curiosity and compassion at the ravaged look on his face.

He exhaled, as if resigned. "My sons."

She barely heard the words, but they stung as surely as if he'd thrown them like stones.

Sons? Automatically, her gaze went to his rough hands, but she already knew he wasn't wearing a ring.

"I didn't know you were…taken," she said, trying not to feel like the world's biggest fool.

Her fingers felt out of place on his arm. Even if he wasn't showing outward signs of belonging to another woman, was he still chained to a ring around his heart? Was that why he'd been so cool to her all this time? Was that why he hadn't pursued things when she'd kissed him?

When she pulled back, his hand captured hers, enfolded her fingers in his. Felicia hitched in a breath, confused.

"Don't, please," he said. "Jenna and I have been divorced for years. A lifetime. She got married again to a man who was there when I couldn't be. They're not a part of my existence anymore."

Her doubts came back to attack her. "You don't see your sons? No visitation?"

You don't like children? Is that why Bobby makes you draw into yourself so much?

"No visitation," he said, going silent.

Ah. Right. Naturally, her last cowboy wouldn't want any more kids. Wasn't that how Felicia's life worked? A splash of hope followed by a flood of disappointment?

She tried not to recognize her folly, but she'd invested so much finger-crossing in Jack, had really thought he'd be the answer to her problems.

Yet, once again, she'd been wrong.

So why was every cell of her body crying out for him? Why was her skin tingling against his as he held her hand?

Overcome, she lost strength, extracting her grip from his, hiding the threat of tears by averting her face.

"And that's it?" she said. Why did her voice have to quaver? Couldn't she pull herself together? She'd done it so often in the past it shouldn't be a problem.

"There's more. A lot more."

She heard the dried leaves stir as he moved closer.

He turned her to meet him, his eyes like the burned remains of a destroyed world, his hands gripping her shoulders a little too tightly.

"My boys…" He stopped. Started again. "They're dead."

She flinched. A sucker punch.

"God, Jack. God. I'm so sorry."

How could he have lived through it?

Clearly, he'd hardened himself. All that was left of his emotion was a sheen of moisture dampening the ashes in his gaze.

"It happened years ago."

"But it still hurts like yesterday." She tilted her head, wanting to take all that pain away from him because she knew she could handle it herself, had spent years handling the loss of children. Sadness was a sharp welt in the back of her throat, making words difficult but necessary. "Does Rip know?"

"No one does. Not around these parts." He looked her in the eye. "No one but you."

His tone had gone a little dead, as if numbing himself were the only way he'd endure.

Just one brief explosion of anguish, just one glimpse into the real Jack, and now she was cut off from him?

He continued, hands slipping down to her upper arms. "These last few days, I've been going back and forth on whether to tell you or not, but… Hell, I can talk to you real easy, Felicia. You listen like you care."

"I do."

A tear slid down her cheek and Jack pressed a hand over it, cradling her face. She rubbed against his coarse skin, soothed.

If only he knew how much she cared.

"Can you tell me what happened?" she whispered.

He exhaled, seemingly allowing every day of grief to escape. "Jenna went to the theater with a friend that night, some kind of musical thing with people running around in rags and moaning about their lives. That wasn't for me, so I stayed home with the boys. An all-guy sports-watching night. My mind wasn't on the games, though. I kept thinking about how much I'd get for a yearling one of my prize stallions had sired."

"You bred horses." She imagined another Jack in another time. A family man with a wife and two boys who ate dinner in a wallpapered room and went to bed after kissing the kids good-night.

Picturing him living with another woman made Felicia cringe, but made her sort of happy, too, because he'd been normal. So much less tortured.

He was still talking, voice flat. "The boys were still real young. Three and five, rascals, a real handful."

A heart-wrenching smile lit over his face and, in that moment, Felicia knew that this man *did* love children, that he'd loved his own to the point where it had made him the walking dead.

She could fall for a man with that sort of power to love, couldn't she? Could give him the will to live again, to want more children.

Couldn't she?

His hands skimmed lower over her arms until he took her hands in his, grasp firm and desperate, touch revealing so much more than his monotone speech did.

"After the game, the kids talked me into putting some frozen fries into the oven and staying up past their bedtime to watch their favorite DVD."

His hands were growing damp.

"We ate," he said, "and I got sleepy during the movie. I'd seen it a thousand times. *Toy Story.* So I wandered off to the bedroom, thinking I'd lay back and rest my eyes while going over our yearly ranch profits in my head. The boys ended up falling asleep in front of the TV." He paused, a muscle flexing in his jaw, his grip tightening on her hands. "And I didn't remember I'd left that oven on."

She couldn't talk, didn't want to. Dying by fire was a horror she couldn't fathom, a blazing trap that turned her stomach in helpless nausea.

He rushed on, the story having gone too far to stop now. "The alarms didn't go off, and the boys were right near the kitchen…. God, I couldn't even get to them, even though I tried and tried. Could only hear them yelling for me—"

Eyes squeezed closed, Jack turned away from her, disconnecting their hands.

He tried to shut out the images of Leroy and Lucas's final moments, but guilt clobbered him, forcing him to invent the scenario anyway. It was all a part of the revolving nightmare, his never-ending penance.

"It was an accident, Jack."

Felicia's voice was like a lifeline, curling into the smoke of his misery to save him.

But he didn't want the reprieve. He didn't deserve it. Remorse was so much a part of his life that turning his back on it didn't seem possible…or even justifiable.

"Accident," he said, the self-hatred as fresh as the water that kept spilling down the creek bed, never stopping to rest or mist away. "I could have changed the damned alarm batteries. I could have woken up earlier. I could have *remembered*."

"Could have."

He felt her fingers on his back and he eased up, wanting so badly to melt under her touch. Wanting to forgive himself just as easily as she would no doubt forgive him.

"I'd give anything to have a life full of could-haves," she said, her voice so soft, so sad in his ear.

Eyes burning with tears that just wouldn't come, he turned to her, saw that she was crying…for him?

Or was there more to it?

At any rate, he didn't deserve her pity. "I'd give my soul for that kind of life, too. But that's not how it works, is it? Because instead of second chances, I've got an ex-wife who left me because she said I'd become a stranger. She told me it wasn't my fault. But I'd catch her watching me with something behind her eyes—blame, I eventually found out. One day, when she couldn't take our quiet spells anymore, she let me have it. Said she was wrong for feeling this way, but that it was my fault. Said that the boys would've woken up in time if they'd heard an alarm, or everything would have been fine if I'd stayed awake." Jackson nodded. Bitter. So damned bitter. "I couldn't help but agree with her. And that's no way to play out a marriage."

He risked a glance at Felicia, wondering if she saw the same careless bastard that Jenna had finally admitted to recognizing.

This woman's never going to look at me again with that light in her eyes. But it's a good thing she knows about me now rather than later.

Yet he detected sympathy, not accusation.

Didn't she get it? Couldn't she grasp the weight of his responsibility?

"You've got to stop this," she said, streaks of red marking her face where the tears had traveled.

When he didn't answer, she pointed a finger into his chest. "Why are you looking at me like that? Did you tell me all this to 'unburden' yourself…or was it to chase me away?"

He couldn't meet her gaze anymore. Maybe that *had* been his primary motive. Maybe he hadn't ever wanted anything from Felicia but a validation of his worthlessness.

Maybe he enjoyed wallowing in self-disgust too much and she was just a new way to do it.

"Ah. Right." She shook her head. "I guess it's option B then. Chase Felicia away."

"No." The word was out before he could rein it in. "You're a sweet woman, and I don't want to see you get hurt when it comes to trying to win me over. You've made your intentions about me clear, and I thought I'd do the same for you."

Liar.

A tiny part of him had been wishing for absolution and he damned well knew it. Because from the moment he'd first seen her, he'd known that Felicia Markowski was his renewal, a light in a sanctuary's window.

A spring of hope that might renew him.

Wrong. He couldn't accept such a load of BS. As if she was going to save him, pump up his soul with sunlight and brightness, snatch him from the jaws of accountability.

Doubtful.

"Hey," he said, as she shook her head and started

to walk away. "I've made a habit of going from ranch to ranch for years, Felicia. Just in case you should come to the Hanging R one day for Bobby and I'm not there, I wanted you to know why."

"I get it," she said. "Ranch to ranch, never settling down, always running. Never getting close enough for anyone to ask a lot of questions. Is that it?"

He shrugged. It would have to suffice as a nod, because she was right and it was too hard to admit it.

"Dammit, Jack, you make me want to scream. What can I do to get through to you?"

A woman who took care to pepper her speech with words like *doggonit* had to feel pretty strongly to be using words like *damn*. Perversely, it bolstered him, showed him how much she really must have cared to be so angry.

"Felicia—"

She held up a hand, wiped away her tears with the other one. "Don't *Felicia* me. Listen, I feel for you. You'll never know how much, either, because you're so closed off to the possibility of someone actually accepting you—faults and all—that it scares you to death."

Before he could catch himself, he'd raised his eyebrows in surprise at her astuteness. But why? He'd always known Felicia was as smart as a whip.

Deep inside, he'd just been hoping she'd see past his shortcomings. That she'd like him enough to wipe away the debris of his self-derision, patiently making him see things clearly again.

She was still worked up right properly. Word by word, hope grew inside of him. Word by word, he started to suspect how much she was coming to mean to him.

"How long has your mourning lasted?" she said. "A few years? More?"

Too many. The boys would've been eleven and nine now. Goddamn.

She seemed so disappointed. "It's become your life."

Shame suffused his skin but, damn, he felt relieved. Finally.

"Listen," she said, her gaze softening along with her tone, "I'm doing everything I can to understand you. But…I don't think you want me to."

What he wanted was to pull her into his arms, to bury his face in her hair, to accept all she had been offering.

But the time it took to imagine the riches of her touch cost him.

With a final-straw shake of her head, she said, "Okay. Got it. Just…" She sighed. "Just know that I'll be around, fool that I am."

When she started to leave again, she added one last thing over her shoulder.

"But, mind you, I won't be around forever."

The crunch of leaves under her shoes faded until he was left alone among the peace of the trees, chastised.

Chapter Nine

It was the longest afternoon of Felicia's life.

Not only was Jack's story tearing at her, but thoughts of her epic hear-me-roar speech in the park were stretching the minutes into eternities, too.

She'd basically challenged him to make the next move, to be the one to pursue *her* now. But would he do it?

Based on his track record, Felicia doubted it very highly.

Even now, at a quarter to midnight, she couldn't get to sleep, too mired in images of Jack's sons to find any peace. Too concerned about Jack to let it go.

Fidgety, she sought the remote on the nightstand by her bed and clicked on the small TV while a fan whisked around and around, stirring the sheets tangled around her legs. She wasn't in the mood for comedy, bad movies or action-show reruns, but she surfed back and forth between them nonetheless. Anything to take her mind off everyone else's troubles.

When she heard a soft knocking at her door, she initially thought it was a sound effect from a cop show. But then it came again, louder, and she froze.

Not even Emmy or Carlota came calling past midnight, so who…?

Heart thudding, she muted the TV and crept to the door, scooping up her cell phone on the way. There weren't many robbers who were polite enough to knock before breaking and entering, but still, the phone felt good in her hand.

"Who is it?" she asked through the wood.

"Jackson."

Felicia almost speared through the roof. What in the world was this about?

Easing open the door, she glimpsed him through the crack. He had his hat in his hands, hair mussed up, making him look vulnerable. Making Felicia want to take him in and hug him right up.

A reluctant teddy bear in need of cuddling. Boy, he'd hate that.

"Hi," he said.

"Hi." Her greeting was longer, pulling one syllable into a few, questioning him with this one tentative word.

Jack shifted position, restless. "I've been thinking about what you said today. Thinking a whole lot."

He'd come all the way over here to tell her that? A *tweeng* of sexual awareness vibrated through her.

"Thinking? About which part exactly?" She was testing him, too reluctant to believe he'd dropped by for something more than casual chatter.

But…gosh, was it ever about time he got the hint.

"All of what you said rattled me to the bone, pretty much," he said.

Oh, boy. She wasn't going to mess this up: Jack, just popping by the neighborhood at an odd hour.

And it wasn't to borrow a cup of sugar, either.

She lowered her eyelashes, smiled, hoping it would work like a charm. "If you were thinking about the part where I said I'd 'be here,' I meant during regular hours, Jack. But now that you're here and it appears I've been keeping you awake, too…"

His eyes traveled from her face to her bare shoulder, where her nightgown strap was on display in the limited view the door crack was offering.

When his gaze darkened, smoldered, coasted right back up to her eyes, she recognized a longing so fierce that her pulse flashed.

Not that she was going to give him the milk before he bought the cow, but she wanted him inside her cottage. That way, it would be harder for him to escape. Then, she could make more of that hard-earned progress, romancing him little by little, just enough to make him leave wanting more. Soon, maybe he'd even fall in love with her and then...

She opened the door.

He took in the full length of her, his shoulders lifting with a caught breath. Crossing her mental fingers, she allowed him to gaze, imagining what he was seeing:

A woman with a few too many pounds around the hips with her blond hair raining over her back. A knee-length nightgown, pure white, covering the silhouette of her curves. Her bare feet tipped with pink-painted toenails.

A package in demure wrapping waiting to be opened.

"You coming in?" she asked.

He lifted an eyebrow, flapped his hat against his thigh. "I'd sure like to."

"But...?" She knew exactly why he was hesitating. Crossing the threshold with her standing here in a nightgown was an admission. A quiet way of saying he wanted more than just walks in the woods.

"Maybe you've got a robe?" he asked, sounding like he hoped she didn't.

"Maybe you should've thought of that before

you came around during the dead of night," she said playfully.

"Maybe I did."

That rugged smile lit over his lips and Felicia's skin flushed. Were they actually bantering?

Progress!

She walked away, luring him inside. Sure enough, he took the bait, closing the door behind himself, keeping his hat by his side as he took measure of her cottage: the framed dime-store pictures of Paris and Venice on her walls, the crocheted doily that had gone half-finished this evening, a closed journal on the top of her nightstand with a pen marking the entry she'd written last night, the bright floral print of her bedspread.

Their gazes met after he finished perusing *that* particular item. There was something different about him tonight, something that told her he wasn't backing away as easily as usual.

But then he blinked and fixed his sights on the TV. Back to being the polite, standoffish Jack.

"Here." She took his hat, anxiously tossed it on an empty chair in front of a mirrored vanity table where she kept perfume and makeup. "Make yourself at home. Want a drink? Water, soda…?"

"Water's good."

He sat in a stuffed recliner that her parents used to own before they passed on. All the furniture she had—their furniture—had been midsixties chic, acquired during their first years of marriage. They'd given birth to Felicia during their last-chance autumn years and had left the world much too soon for her liking. She'd been their "miracle baby," their sunshine, and she'd loved them back just as fiercely.

After Felicia got two bottles of water from her minifridge, she stood in front of him, too excited to sit down.

"So…" She smiled, took a sip.

"So." Jack hadn't even cracked his beverage open yet. Instead, he thumped the plastic bottle against his leg, just like he'd done with his hat. "I suppose I should explain."

"Mmm-hmm."

He stopped with the leg-whacking, met her curious gaze straight on. "You've put up with a lot from me, and when you walked away this afternoon, it felt like there was a thread left hanging."

"And you decided to snip it off tonight."

"In a manner of speaking. I couldn't sleep, and I wondered if you'd gone to bed thinking that I didn't give a damn about what you said today."

Felicia had been in the middle of lifting the bottle to her lips again, but at his confession, she slowly lowered it.

He continued. "What I'm trying to say is sorry. I'm sorry for being such a gruff jerk."

Dust off his words a little and Felicia got a glimpse of what they really could be:

His way of saying he wanted to be with her?

Or was she reading too much into this midnight visit?

Because…duh.

This was *so* Jack. Roundabout, enigmatic, taking the hard way around things when they could be done more directly. But that was what made him such an out-of-the-ordinary man.

That was why she'd tripped head over heels for him.

Felicia set her bottle down on the nearest flat surface—the TV stand—and smoothed out her nightdress. He followed the progress of her hands, the way they were touching her body in such an innocuous way—but not really.

She wasn't blind to the growing hunger in the center of his gaze. She liked it, took great pleasure in stoking it.

"In actuality, you're not so gruff," she said, her voice a little urgent, foreign.

"Not so much around you. Not anymore." Even *he* sounded strangled. "You do something to me, Felicia, but hell if I know what it is. I just wish I could do the same to you."

She jerked, coming to watch him from the corner of her eye in a narrowed glance. Was he talking about the way she comforted him? And he wanted to…comfort her?

"There's just…" His forehead furrowed. "You seem sad at times. Like you understand me a little too well."

And there it was again—the nearly imperceptible web of hurt that strung them together. Slender, almost a mirage in its fragility, but strong enough to capture all the small details.

God, she just wanted to lean down where he was sitting and touch him, to make contact so she would know she wasn't dreaming this up out of pure desperation.

Holding her breath, she reached out, smoothed a stray lock of dark-and-silver hair away from his temple. He closed his eyes, molding his hand over hers, singeing her.

"Just being around you…" he murmured, angling his lips against her wrist, pressing his mouth there until his five-o'clock shadow scratched and burned against her sensitive skin.

The kiss was soft, his mouth moist and warm. Felicia started to keen for the want of him low in her belly. The sensation spiraled downward, twisting between her legs, making her tremble, lose strength and shift forward until her knees were against his. She braced herself from falling by levering her other hand on the back of the chair.

The linen nightgown gaped away from her body, brushed over his face as the fan whipped air over them. It made her feel half-naked, sensual, yet at the same time fearful.

The physical pain of being with him, she thought. What if it hurt as much as that first time?

But the notion was just a strike of lightning in the storm of her mind, passion sheeting over her as Jack kept kissing her wrist, her palm. When he slid his hands into the small of her back, Felicia gasped, responding by slumping the rest of her weight onto the chair and straddling him.

With a groan of surrender, he used her nightgown to tug her the rest of the way down, running one hand up her back and into her hair, pulling her to him for a long, searing kiss.

They took up where they'd left off days ago near the barn, greedily sipping at each other, her fingers sweeping through his hair, too, craving more.

His mouth broke away from hers for an instant. "Come here," he said, one set of fingers cupping her rear end, urging her closer, closer, until her breasts were flush against him.

Jackson's head swam, body tightening at the feel of her beaded nipples against his chest. With something close to a growl, he resumed their kiss, deepened it, sliding his tongue into her mouth, exploring, tasting, enjoying this too damned much.

She felt lighter than clouds, smelled a little like heaven, too, with her long hair tickling his cheek and her nightie belling away from her body. Earlier, he'd seen the shadow of her lush figure through the white of the material, had just about lost his mind right there and then.

You couldn't stay away from her, could you? he asked himself. *"I'm sorry for being such a jerk,"* indeed.

Dammit, it was true that he really had come to care about what she thought of him, but he was almost ashamed of inventing such a lame excuse to be here expressing it, making out with the furious need of a teenage boy in lust for the first time.

Truthfully, should he even be here at all?

When they came up for air, panting, he sketched his fingers up her smooth arms, under the straps of her gown, toying with the linen. A bit lower, he could see the outline of her stimulated breasts under the nightie.

So close he could lean his head forward and take them into his mouth. So perfect he wanted to feel them in his hands, meld them into his memory.

He looked up at her, his breath chopping out of him, his blood simmering, building into an inferno.

"You've got a way of putting me just right," he managed to say.

"Jack." Her cheeks were pink, making her eyes shine all the brighter. "Don't stop now."

But he should. Really, really should. Even though she had him feeling so good, he could sense the inevitable guilt lying just below the surface of his flesh, gnawing there and waiting its turn. In fact, the longer they weren't doing something as mind-boggling as kissing, the easier it was to return to his doubts.

Then kiss her again, you dunderhead, said his better instincts.

She shyly laid a hand on his shirt, fiddling with a button. He relaxed his head against the chair's cushion, heartbeat banging, watching her, turned on by the grace of her hands, the yearning in her wide gaze.

Today, he'd told her not to be surprised if she discovered the ranch to be empty of him at some point. And he hadn't been kidding, either. But after taking one gander at her in a nightgown, he'd decided that maybe he'd *actually* come over here to convince himself that he needed to stay in Wycliffe. For a long time.

Maybe forever, whatever that meant.

But could he really sit here and say that he was ready to make a commitment like that? To a woman he'd known for such a short time?

Jackson wasn't a believer in destiny—not by a long shot—so how could he explain these feelings he was struggling with?

Felicia worked his first button loose, drawing her fingers down to the next.

Jeez, he needed to stop her. Soon.

He'd rested his hands on her thighs and now, with her undressing him, his digits inadvertently clawed as he fought himself. Her nightgown bunched in his fists, revealing more pale skin to his famished gaze.

She undid another button.

What if he went and fell in love with Felicia?

She loosened another.

No, he couldn't deal with affection again, that was the bottom line. It wouldn't be fair to anyone, making them live with all his demons.

So how could he sit here and let Felicia think it could happen? He knew what she wanted from him—the whole kit and caboodle. Things that a woman like her deserved.

In the end, how could he take advantage of her youth and willingness merely so he could feel like a man again?

"I'm glad you came over here tonight," she said, slipping her fingers beneath his shirt.

She traced over his abs, his chest, gently circling his nipples, cautiously stimulating them, as if curious about how a man worked.

It was as if someone had taken a sledgehammer to his head. His body rang with an inner wake-up alarm, tremors quavering up and down his skin, bringing the lower half of him to attention.

He knew she could feel his arousal beneath her,

because she got a beatific look on her face, her lips going into a pleased O.

When she shifted over him, a tiny grind of further exploration, Jackson sucked in a breath, planted his hands on her hips, arched slightly into her. Damn, she felt good. And when she made a tiny mewling sound, she felt even better.

"Felicia, that's something you don't do to a man unless you mean it," he said, pulling back, his groin protesting with pressure beyond imagination.

He bit back a curse, knowing he'd earned every second of frustration. Knowing exactly what she would say next.

Her thumbs went back to circling his nipples. "What makes you think I'm only fooling around?"

Couldn't she go back to being that prairie sweetheart who seemed so virginal? She was *killing* him.

Or maybe he didn't want her to revert at all.

For Pete's sake, what did he want? He was so screwed up even a whole toolbox couldn't set him back to rights.

He captured her hands in his, just to calm things down for the time being. "Hold up, sweetheart."

She flashed a smile at the endearment, but then, after a long second, her face fell, shoulders sinking in realization.

"It's not working for you?" she asked.

"No, I wouldn't say that at all." He massaged her

hands, not wanting her to feel that his reluctance was her fault. It was his. All of it.

She laughed, a delicate, pained sound that about broke Jackson's heart.

"Well, I thought I was doing something to your libido," she said. "And rightly so, because you're supposed to be my fate. My future."

His head banged against the back of his chair as he lost muscle control. Fate? Him?

And how had she known he'd been thinking about something real similar only moments ago?

She rushed on. "I've been debating about telling you something, and I think what I've got to say just might make me the nation's biggest fruitcake. Still…"

After a pause, she intertwined her fingers with his, then told him about an empath psychic friend named Carlota and how she'd predicted Felicia would have a baby with someone called "the last cowboy."

What? Of all the…

Wait. Besides the lunacy of this, could it be that she was just pursuing him to make this crazy prophecy come true? Was that all he was to her?

She must've read the question in his face because she was quick to say, "I didn't believe it myself, either, even if I really, truly wanted to. All I knew is that one look at you made me a goner, Jack. And now, every passing day, I just want to believe what Carlota said more and more."

Not even Jackson could deny the strike of desire he'd felt when he'd first met Felicia. Relief burrowed into him, welcome and surprising.

Still, the whole thing sounded like a stretch, even if he suspected Carlota was the fortune-teller he'd literally run into at the charity event.

Had her friend touched him and gotten some kind of reading at that moment?

Yeah, sure. And the cow jumped over the moon.

"We've already talked about this cowboy thing," he said. "And I'm not one of them."

Something in Felicia's gaze closed, like a box of dreams being taped up for storage. "I know. You're not a cowboy, and…" She swallowed. "And I'm probably not going to be having children anyway."

She'd said it with such deceptive blandness that Jackson wondered if he'd heard the words correctly.

The air had changed around them. It was no longer sultry, with a fan blowing warm breezes around their bodies. It was clipped now, as efficient as a wind you needed to turn your coat collar against.

She made her way off his lap, leaving him empty as she tidied her nightgown, then her hair. Sitting on the bed, she faced him, as straightforward as always.

But even though the temperature of the room had changed, the thermometer in his body had stayed the same—overheated. And staring at her like an addled fool wouldn't cool him down, either.

"The doctors can define my problem much better than I can," she said, her posture a little too upright. "I developed something called endometriosis."

Sounded serious. He started forward in his chair, consumed by the bad news, stomach knotting up.

"No, Jack, it's not like I'm on my deathbed." She smiled at him, calm, accepting. "There's some tissue that grew outside my uterus, where it shouldn't have strayed, and it attacked my reproductive organs."

Jackson's instinct to protect her overrode the typical male need to shrink back at the too-much-information female talk.

Felicia. His sweet cheerleading squad of one, hiding her pain and not wanting him to comfort her. He felt bereft, left out in the dark because he wanted to help her and she didn't seem to need it.

"Is there anything to be done about it?" he asked.

"I'm scheduled for laser surgery in a few months, but they tell me the symptoms are likely to reoccur afterward. But then there're other options that might allow me to have children. Superovulation, intra-uterine insemination. Nothing's a cure-all."

One glance around her quaint cottage told him that a maid from Oakvale probably wouldn't be able to afford such treatment beyond what insurance might pay.

She noticed his assessment, sent him a look that hinted she'd thought about it, also.

But—this was the thing of it—she didn't seem beaten down. In fact, she'd even set out to make this crazy prediction, this so-called answer to her troubles come true.

So she thought *he* could be the one to give her a child instead of some expensive cure?

Even if it was physically possible, he didn't know about the emotional part. Another little boy or girl. Another kid who might leave him too early.

Jackson didn't know if he could survive that.

But…

A thought occurred to him, a tremor of suspicion.

If Felicia couldn't have children, wouldn't that make her the perfect woman for him?

Could he stand to find out? Because Jenna had shut him down, as well. The brusque nature he'd developed wasn't just about Leroy and Lucas.

Felicia had been quietly watching the emotions play over him. He could tell by the melancholy understanding on her face.

"Didn't I say it was slightly unbelievable?" she asked.

Unbelievable? Hell, he was feeling things for her that he hadn't felt for another woman in…well, ever. He'd loved Jenna, but he wasn't so sure it'd been so passionately, or even with this weird invisible cable that seemed to connect him and Felicia.

But…fate? Impossible.

"I'm not into magic," he said gently. "All I know is that I'm lucky that you even care to lay eyes on me."

She seemed right pleased at that. "Really? Even though…?"

Her hands moved around near her stomach, searching for a way to end the question.

"What?" he asked.

She stopped, staring at him incredulously. "You don't appear to be so taken aback by my news, Jack. People haven't been as accepting of this in the past."

How could he tell her what he was feeling without seeming selfish? How could he explain that no babies was the only option for him when she so obviously adored children and would make such a wonderful mother?

"People haven't been accepting, you say?" The lightbulb was finally going off in his head. "You mean ex-boyfriends, like the one you were talking about in Rip's kitchen?"

"You got it. Seems a lot of men want a family, and I can't blame them for needing a woman who can provide that."

"But…" He stood. "You're worth much more, Felicia. Hasn't anyone noticed?"

She looked away and bit down on her lips, a very feminine precursor to tears, in Jackson's experience.

How could anyone have ever rejected her?

More to the point, how could *he?*

His comments seemed to have taken root in her, flowering into confidence as she burst into the biggest smile he'd seen yet. It nearly knocked him over with its brilliant power.

"Thank you," she whispered, her eyes moist. "But just so you know, I aim to make you see that I can give you everything, too." She gave a cute shrug. "Carlota's never wrong."

Though he doubted her optimism, he kept his tongue, sitting back down in his chair because he didn't feel it was the time to leave.

Aw, hell, he would admit it. He just didn't want to go.

For the next couple of hours, they relaxed with each other, talked about her family, his family, opening up more by the minute, because what secrets were left to tell?

Jackson could pinpoint one, he thought, after kissing Felicia good-night under her porch lamp.

She certainly wouldn't appreciate knowing that he never intended to have children at all.

Last cowboy or not.

Chapter Ten

The following week was a lovely blur for Felicia, consisting of visits to the Hanging R, post-dinner quality hanging-out time with Bobby…

…and post-Bobby quality alone time with Jack.

Ever since the night he'd come to her cottage, they'd been seeing each other, kissing under the moonlight, holding hands as the stars blazed down on them. She hadn't intended to tell him about her infertility so early on, but it'd obviously been the right choice. Surprisingly, the revelation had seemed to sway him *toward* her instead of away, unlike what had happened with the rest of her boyfriends.

Just imagine—her last cowboy had been the first man to ever take the news decently.

It was the last thing she would have predicted.

And the second-to-last thing was the way Jack had managed to get into Bobby's good graces. Not that the wrangler was overextending himself in this area. No, ironically, all Jack had to do was be around and Bobby would gravitate toward his general area, both of them sitting near each other wordlessly while Jack whittled on the sly and Bobby colored pictures with the markers and paper Felicia had bought him.

The sight touched her, but stymied her just the same.

Didn't Bobby know that Jack had kid issues?

More importantly, didn't Jack himself even know?

Felicia was asking herself these kinds of needless questions a few nights later, when she suggested to Carlota that they take a few Oakvale boys and girls— children of their friends and fellow house workers— to the rodeo and out for a burger afterward.

"You know Toby's going to be there," Carlota said.

"I don't mind," Felicia answered. "My ex-boyfriends can be wherever they want. Besides, Bobby's all fired up to see a rodeo. He's never been to one before."

Thus, a plan was born, made all the better after Jack said he would go with them.

Even with all those kids there.

Was he getting more comfortable around them?

Felicia would have to spy closely tonight, just to see what was going on.

It turned out that all of them—six Oakvale children, Bobby, Felicia, Jack and Carlota—enjoyed the festivities, the red, white and blue bunting around the arena, the calf roping, bull riding and barrel racing. Toby Baker even fell off his bull after two seconds, adding a decidedly poetic sense of justice to the proceedings.

As the kids munched on salted peanuts and cheered as Toby scrambled to his feet, chaps flying away from his legs in his haste, Jack kept shaking his head.

"I've seen longer staying time with a frog popping on a skillet," he said. He hadn't been too ecstatic to find out that Felicia's ex was in town anyway; this just gave him an excuse to vent.

She tried not to smile at Jack's apparent jealousy as Toby hightailed it back behind the barrier, his horned foe in hot pursuit as a rodeo clown attempted to distract the animal.

Instead, she latched her pinkie through Jack's, watched his face grow ruddy in acknowledgment.

This was enough for her right now, she thought, holding pinkies with him in public. Soon she would make him love her so much that he wouldn't be shy about kissing her in the middle of a crowded Wycliffe sidewalk.

Soon.

Because, after all, progress was being made.

Content for the moment, Felicia smiled at Carlota, who was sitting in the middle of all the children, eating just as many cotton candies and churros. She turned around, giving a discreet nod toward Felicia and Jack's linked pinkies, looking pretty darned smug at the evidence of another prediction going right.

Felicia winked at her and Carlota went back to making sure Michael Henry didn't stuff himself too full before dinner and that Cissy Duarte wasn't fretting about the doll she'd gotten dirty when she'd dropped it below the bleachers and Jack had retrieved it for her.

Then Felicia's gaze settled on Bobby, who was sitting right below them. He was jumping up and down, as active as any six-year-old, excited about the rodeo and the fact that he'd met new friends tonight. Joel and Noel Tate, sons of a fellow Oakvale housekeeper. The platinum-headed twins were a couple of years older and wiser, so Felicia was keeping her eye on the spirited boys.

But Bobby was having a lot of harmless fun, laughing and high-fiving with them. She wasn't about to break up the first peer relationship he was forming in Wycliffe.

After the rodeo, Cissy was heading for a nap and

Joel was starting to throw peanuts at everyone, but they still made their promised stop at the Burger Barn, Wycliffe's greatest and only "soda shop."

The aroma of grilled meat, hot fudge sauce and French fries greeted them as Felicia, Jack and Carlota escorted their charges to a long Formica table with red-cushioned metal chairs. The room bustled with bow-tied waitresses carrying trays of ice creams. Tourists nursed their sunburns while wearing khaki shorts and cameras. Rodeo cowboys sat at the bar, grabbing a snack. A player piano tinkled out ragtime tunes from a corner while a clown carried around a batch of colorful balloons.

Jack seemed distinctly uncomfortable as he took a chair on the far side of Felicia—a seat that assured him some distance from Oakvale's pumped-up kids.

"I'm—" he jammed his thumb toward the door "—thinking it's a good time for a lungful of fresh air."

"No, you don't." Felicia grabbed his hand as if she were going to chain him to the table. "You're mine for the next hour, and Bobby's ride home, to boot."

That smile he'd been developing for the last week and a half claimed him, and Felicia's tummy did the happy dance.

But why couldn't her brain be doing it, too? Why was it nagging at her that even though Jack had come a long way, it wasn't far enough?

Under the table, he slipped his hand into hers and she was assuaged for the moment.

"You know, Jack," she said, "you seem like a natural in this setting. I've always imagined you wearing an arm garter and a striped vest just like the soda jerks."

"And running around the room with my arms full of greasy grub. Believe me, it's a fantasy I've been keeping well hidden."

She laughed. "Careful. Your sense of humor's showing."

"Can't have that."

He squeezed her hand and she scooted her chair just a little closer to his.

There. Near enough to breathe him in.

After ordering, Joel and Noel appointed themselves ringleaders, telling loud, silly jokes only an eight-year-old could appreciate. Or a boy just slightly younger.

Bobby was doing his best to keep up with his new friends, to impress them. But when he turned goof-ball and "accidentally" spilled salt all over himself, Jack motioned the boy over with one crook of his finger. And with a gently quelling glance from Felicia, the twins settled down, too.

From the abashed look on Bobby's face, he knew he was about to get a reminder about how to act in a restaurant—even if it was a madhouse like the Burger Barn.

Jack let go of Felicia's hand, leaving her skin to cool, to feel really lonely without his grip to warm it up.

"Having fun?" Jack said to the curly-headed boy.

Bobby nodded and Felicia brushed the salt from his red-and-white striped top. He sent a little grin to her, owning her heart once again.

"Bob," Jack said, "see your friends down there?"

He gestured toward the blond twins, who seemed perpetually hopped up on sugar with those rubber-faced expressions they were making at each other.

"Yes," Bobby said.

"You want people to go around with that sort of image of you for the rest of their days?" Jack asked, his tone mild. "Or do you want them to have respect for you? Because sometimes, what people see is what people get. You understand what I'm saying? You show them a fool by how you handle yourself and, more than likely, there's a fool to be shown."

Right. What people see is what people get, Felicia thought. Except with Jack himself.

Bobby took another peek at the jokers down the table then turned back to Jack. "If I go around making those kinds of faces, people might think I'm a dork."

Jack gave the boy's hair a fond ruffle, avoiding Felicia's stunned gaze.

"That's right," he said, "and you're no dork."

Seeking a second opinion, Bobby glanced at

Felicia. She rubbed his back in agreement. He was no dork.

"Say…" Jack reached into his jeans pocket, extracted something, wrapped his fingers around whatever it was. "I've got a prize for you."

He held out one of those sticks he'd been whittling at for as long as Felicia could remember. But this particular piece had taken the shape of a rough T. rex dinosaur. It was no work of art, yet at least she could identify it.

"Wow." Bobby took it from Jack, running his index finger over the stumpy tail, the big head, the tiny claws.

When Felicia caught Jack's eye, he looked away. Another blush?

She didn't know what was going on here, but it seemed as if a door had been broken down, allowing her a glimpse into Jack's soul.

He *did* love kids, and it made her wonder all the more when he would allow her to get close enough to start having theirs.

"When I was young," Jack said to Bobby, "I carried around a chunk of wood my dad carved. A totem, he called it, with ugly faces that were supposed to protect me. Now, this isn't much more to look upon, but it should do the same for you, Bob. Look out for you, I mean."

"A T. rex is tough," the boy said. "He won't let anyone mess with me. Thanks, Mr. North."

"You're welcome. A tough totem for a tough guy. Now go show those twins how to act in an eating establishment."

"I will." Bobby started to dash off, then stopped, flashing both Jack and Felicia a huge smile. Then he was gone, immediately showing his treasure to Joel and Noel, who were fascinated. But another watchful glance from Felicia kept them mindful about the consequences of snatching it away from the younger boy.

"That was…" She searched for a word powerful enough to cover what she'd just witnessed. Couldn't think of one.

"Yeah." Jack shrugged off the compliment, grinning from ear to ear nonetheless.

The wood had finally taken form for him, she thought. He'd finally been able to create something special, to give a piece of himself to another person.

Could he ever do the same with her?

"I've got to get that fresh air I was talking about," Jack said, standing, obviously doing his best to downplay his kindness. "This place is battering at my head."

"You do what you need to do," she said, touching his thigh.

She hadn't meant anything sexual by it. She'd only wanted to tell him she would miss him for even the few minutes it would take to pull his alpha genes back together. But a fire in his eyes had been rekindled, and she knew he was thinking of all their kisses and what they had the potential to turn into someday.

If he would only let them.

"I won't be gone long," he said, voice graveled.

"I hope not."

She watched him go, appreciating the way he filled his clothing—from the wide shoulders straining against his shirt to the work-honed butt filling his jeans.

Boy. Jack North. The biggest mystery this side of heaven.

As she chatted about "tough animals" with Joel, Noel and Bobby, the parents of three of the children met them for dinner, as planned. She and Carlota had already agreed to take home the twins and Cissy Duarte, so that left Bobby in Jack's care. All accounted for.

Then their waitress brought their burgers, but Felicia merely poked at hers, hungry for something much more substantial than food. Jack hadn't been gone for more than ten minutes and she was already yearning for him as if he was dessert.

Well, she might as well take advantage of his absence and make a washroom run to freshen up.

She signaled to Carlota about where she was going, then got out of her chair, her purse in tow so she could use lipstick and run a comb through her hair.

And that was when she saw him. Toby Baker, laughing with his friends near the entrance while they waited for a table.

Wonderful.

It was too late to go back to the kids, where she felt so comfortable and needed. So instead, fate decreed that Toby catch sight of her as his group was seated at a table near the front windows. It ordained that he tell his friends he would be along in a minute.

Zero choice in the matter, she told herself that Toby was just like any of her other exes and walked over to him.

"Good to see you," she said, half meaning it. She couldn't hold a grudge against any of her exes. Life was too short to play those sorts of games and bringing herself down to such a petty level wasn't appealing to her. But she would get out of this just as soon as was polite.

"Good to see you, too, Felicia." Hat off, he revealed shaggy blond hair.

He'd obviously showered and changed after his bout at the rodeo, but nothing had washed away the memory of how he'd treated her. Fighting it, Felicia still couldn't overcome the deadening of her self-esteem all over again, couldn't help reliving the awkward look on his face after she'd told him her painful secret.

A hint of that rejection was hiding in his gaze right now.

Funny how Carlota and Emmy had first thought Toby was Felicia's last cowboy. If they'd known how he'd treated her, they would have hunted him down and smacked him silly. But Felicia believed in being kind to all manner of God's creatures.

Including animals.

As they stared at each other in toe-tapping silence, Felicia held back the need to tell him a thing or two.

I know a man who could care less about my condition. His name is Jack. He's my future. And he'll never treat me the way you did.

But was that true?

"You look great," Toby finally said. "How've you been?"

"Wonderful. And you?"

Another party of tourists walked through the front door and Toby moved to the side, grasping her elbow to guide her with him.

No tingle. No heat.

"Fine," he said, "even if I'm not managing eight seconds in my event, but other than that, life is good."

"I'm glad to hear it."

Wow. This man had wanted to go to "the next level" with her a couple of months ago and now they could barely manage a conversation.

"I could be *much* better in some areas, though," he said, smiling at her and using all the charm that had made her like him in the first place.

Felicia got a bad vibe from that smile.

Was he hitting on her? Had her infertility changed her from marriage material into some kind of buckle bunny who wasn't worth more than a tumble in a run-down motel room?

Or was she reading too much into this, as usual?

She decided to take the high road. "I'll let you get back to your friends now. Best of luck."

The door opened again to let more people inside, and the crowd pushed her and Toby backward.

"God, Felicia." He stared down at her, looking genuinely sorry. "Do you know I can't get to sleep some nights because of how things turned out?"

Was this the apology she'd been waiting for?

He continued. "I keep thinking, if things had only been different…"

He stopped there and she didn't move, still waiting.

And waiting.

Was that *it?*

"Different?" she asked.

"You know." He used his hat to motion to her stomach. "Your problem."

"Problem?" She chuffed, all her frustration coming out in that one I'm-about-to-turn-into-the-Hulk sound. "You mean," she whispered, just to make her point, *"endometriosis?"*

He shrugged, the womanly issue forcing him to look as if he wanted to shrivel into himself.

"Thanks for the explanation, Toby. You really improved my opinion of you."

She tried to get away again, but her ex hitched on to her arm.

"Let's talk about this…."

A deep, angry voice interrupted him.

"Let go of her."

Jack, his gaze dark and livid, parted the bodies behind Toby and pointed at the bull rider's grip on Felicia.

"Let go means *let go,*" he reiterated.

Toby complied, holding up his hands in sheepish surrender. "Done."

"Now get." Jack sounded as if he were talking to a bad dog.

Toby sent her a glance now. Yeah, like she was going to ask him to stay.

"You need me to tell you to scram with a phone call?" Felicia asked.

Cringing at the reference to how he'd broken up with her, Toby backed off, going to join his friends.

He never was a fighter, Felicia thought. And not actually a lover, either.

Jack seemed as if he was about to go after him.

"He's not worth it," Felicia said, too drained to put much energy into explaining everything.

"What he said to you…" Jack fisted his hands. "I could hear every word from where I was standing."

"It's nothing. Forget about him. I already have."

Ha. Even now she was still stinging from the reopened wounds.

Resting his hands on her arms, Jack came around to face her. There was such care in the way he held her, such restrained anger about what she had to live with.

"I'll go in there and get Bobby so I can take the two of you home now," he said.

"But Carlota was going to see to that."

"She can handle three kids from what I've witnessed. Besides, I… Well, the night's still young."

She could tell he wanted to be with her, soothe her, and that was okay in her book. Any time she could steal with him was good time.

"Don't go messing with Toby on your way to get Bobby," she said, meaning it.

"Me?" Jack tried to look harmless as he gave her arms one last rub. "I'm coming right back."

She watched him go, a lump in her throat.

He would come back. But how long would it be before he stayed away for good?

After helping Rip tuck Bobby into bed at the Hanging R, Jackson drove Felicia back to Oakvale, taking the winding back roads past streams lined by cottonwood and oak trees, past meadows and high ridges shadowed by the night.

He'd been so very proud of himself for not back-handing that pseudocowpoke back at the Burger Barn. When Jackson had first come through the door, looked over the heads of the gathered crowd and spotted Toby Baker grinning and making time with Felicia, he'd gotten a little angry.

But then Jackson had come close enough to hear what Felicia's ex had been saying. The disrespect Baker had shown her had been like flint against Jackson's skin, and he'd lost his temper.

It was that simple.

But not really simple at all.

Not when he couldn't sort out these feelings he was having for Felicia. Not when he was having such a hard time coping with everything she was stirring up inside of him.

Right now, Felicia was in the middle of giving him the details about Toby: how they'd met on a Wycliffe sidewalk during last year's rodeo and he'd wooed her right into the Burger Barn for an ice-cream soda. How he'd tried to teach her to rope and how hopeless she'd been at it. How he'd broken up with her on the phone like a coward.

By the time Jackson drove past Oakvale Mansion,

a mammoth house that overlooked the landscape from a hilltop, he was fit to be tied.

"I should've knocked that poke upside the head when I had the chance," he muttered, steering down a lane toward the cottages nestled below the big hill.

"I don't think Toby can sustain much more brain damage." As usual, she was trying to lighten things up. "But he proved one thing to me."

"What's that?"

Jackson pulled in front of Felicia's place, the white planks trimmed with green woodwork and shutters. Hand-painted flowers laced the doorway and windows.

"It proved he's not my last cowboy," she said, "even if he did come in at the bottom of his event."

Last place. *The last cowboy.*

As Jackson cut the engine, the ominous phrase rang in his ears. "That just goes to show you, then. Predictions are best used as compost."

When she didn't respond, he turned to see that she was as stunned as if he'd slapped her. Instinctively, he laid a hand on the back of her head, cradling her.

"You know how I feel about what Carlota said." He stroked her soft strands. "*We* cause everything that happens to us. There's no such thing as a universe that has everything all planned out."

A smile struggled to her lips. "I keep wondering the same thing, Jack, but…"

"You want to believe."

The song of crickets and rustling leaves filled the quiet.

"The thing is," she said softly, "the prediction's not the only thing telling me you're the one. My heart's saying it, too."

Oh, hell. She hadn't just taken the plunge, had she? Was this just an inch away from something much scarier than kissing and enjoying each other's company?

"See," she said. "Look at you, now. You're scared to death, and I can't help second-guessing if all this is right, prediction or not."

"That's because I am…scared."

Phew, he'd said it.

"Jack." She nestled her body closer to his, framing his face in her hands. "We're all scared in some way or another."

But not like him. God help anyone who was as much of a coward as Jackson North was.

He braced himself, knowing now was the time to come clean, to stop fooling both of them into thinking they would get somewhere.

"Felicia," he said, "I'm not looking to have a family."

Even though she drew away, he forced himself to continue.

"Never again."

Chapter Eleven

Felicia pretended she hadn't heard what he'd said.

No family? Never again…?

She just wasn't understanding him correctly, right? Because if Jack was meant to be with her—to give her a child, for heaven's sake—he would eventually crave kids as much as she did. He would yearn to rock them to sleep at night, would take great joy in seeing their first steps, their first smiles.

But that wasn't what was coming out of his mouth.

"Felicia?" he asked, holding her hands, rubbing his thumbs over her skin.

"You don't want a family," she repeated, still in a daze. "That's not part of the plan."

"What plan…? *Felicia.*"

When she met his gaze, her vision was a little fuzzy, as if the world had turned into an out-of-focus movie that required adjustment.

"Listen to me." He seemed so intense, so mired in his own beliefs. "Don't get me wrong. I want you. God, I want you with every screaming molecule of my body. And I don't care if you wouldn't be able to give me children. You're pretty damned wonderful the way you are."

She was so numb she couldn't even enjoy his compliment. "That's all I'd ever be to you? A lover?"

Never a wife.

Never the mother of his children.

He kept hold of her, his resolution seeming to grow while hers only waned.

"I know," he said. "What I offer isn't good enough for you. But it's all I can give. I'm not suited to be a father."

"Look at you and Bobby. You're so good with him…."

"That's different." The past settled between them, thick and heavy with dead wishes. "Bobby belongs to Rip. I'm not responsible for him. I already got a chance with my own family, and I failed."

His words were edged by a self-hatred so profound that Felicia couldn't even answer.

So what was he going to do? she thought. Did he intend to drift from ranch to ranch for the rest of his life, always catching the wind to a place where he could forget Leroy and Lucas?

The idea of him leaving, being an eternal slave to guilt, drilled into her. She gripped his hands, afraid to let go.

"I don't understand you," she said. "Is your remorse really that comfortable, Jack? Or are you afraid to abandon it?"

He glanced down at their linked fingers and she knew she'd hit upon the truth.

How could she compete with it?

She couldn't. Of all the men in the world, her last cowboy had turned out to be a figment of her imagination.

Did this mean she needed to find another willing partner who would finally make her whole? Another candidate who could bring her hopes to fruition? What was she going to—?

No.

With sudden clarity, Felicia realized that her own needs were buried beneath the love that had grown for this man.

Maybe fate had been working on an entirely different scheme when it had sent him her way?

Gently, she used her index finger to tip his chin up, guiding his gaze back to hers.

"For the rest of my life," she whispered, "I'm going to love you no matter what, Jack North."

He seemed confused and elated—struck as helpless as a lone tree under a sky jumping with lightning.

"I'm…" He shook his head.

Liberated by her confession, Felicia moved her fingers to his jaw, cupping it. "You're not sure how to respond. I'm not exactly surprised about that. But it needed to be said. And I'll do it again, too. I love you, Jack, more than anything."

More than even her dreams.

For a second, it looked as if he might have something to tell her, too, but he shut his mouth against the words.

She waited him out, mentally encouraging him, stroking his whisker-bristled cheek and taking in the weathered beauty of him. Underneath the gruff exterior hid a heart so big that it had room for all sorts of affection.

All she had to do was convince him to let her in.

As the night serenaded them, she saw a battle play over his normally stoic features. The obvious need to touch her, the subtle hint of an emotion that lifted her sky high.

Could it have anything to do with love? Maybe, just maybe?

Finally, he spoke. "I'm not much for promises, Felicia."

"I'm not asking for any." Not tonight, at least.

Then again, she thought, hope did spring eternal.

He chuffed softly, giving her a knowing glance from beneath a lowered brow.

"What?" She stepped up her plan for more *progress,* burying her fingers in his hair, toying with it.

"You."

She could tell she was getting to him, his eyelids going heavy with that bedroom look guys fell into when they wanted to lay a kiss on a girl.

"What about me?" she asked, drawing her other hand behind his neck, caressing an uneven hairline that could've used a good trim.

He slid a hand under the hem of her long skirt and over her knee, rubbing. Felicia just about melted, her blood heating and flowing to lava in her veins.

Jack's voice dropped lower. "You're killing me, Felicia."

"You said you wanted me, right?"

He muttered a curse.

Inhaling, cheering herself on, she smoothed one hand down his chest, over the thud of his wildly beating heart. She inched closer, so near she could feel the hush of her words singing over his cheek as she released them.

"I need you, too, Jack, prediction or not."

His grip tightened on her knee as she moved closer still, nestling her lips under his jaw. She pressed tender kisses on his warm, roughened skin, tasting, breathing in the soap and leather and musk of him.

In response, he leaned into her, his other hand sweeping over her hair as he murmured her name.

He said it over and over again, reminding her of a parched man praying for water. While she kissed her way to his cheek, his chin, his lips, she absorbed every *Felicia,* his urgent whispers filling places that had long gone dry.

With her heartbeat fluttering, she shaped her mouth to his, pulling at his lips in slow time, deepening the contact into a head-spinning request for something more.

Between breaths, he talked against her lips. "Every time you do that, it gets harder for me to stop."

"Good."

They paused against each other, heat pouring down her body, coming to rest in her belly where it flexed and moaned to life.

Her need for him hurt, sharp and insistent, a dull ache of pleasure. She could feel herself priming for him, even as her memories reminded her of that first time, when she'd felt ripped apart.

"Hey." He framed her face with his hands. "Change your mind already?"

"Never." She was ready for her future, ready for him to be a part of her life whether he resisted it or not.

Uh-huh. She was ready. Right?

As if to prove it, she melded herself against him, chest to chest.

Forget pain. There's just him. Jack.

Giving in, he repaid her with a languid, demanding kiss, his tongue teasing hers with long, wet strokes. As they devoured each other, he shifted Felicia over the pickup's vinyl seat so she lay beneath him, her feet braced against the driver's door, the bulge in his jeans hard against the center of her.

Ah, there. This was what she'd fantasized about. Sultry kisses, the lulling weight of his body on hers. Moonlight, heavy breathing and vision so dizzy she couldn't see straight.

Even now, as he worked off his shirt then tore it away from his body, she felt like this was all a dream—hazy with so much pure yearning that the fringes of it blurred into another version of reality.

Faintly, she was aware of him tossing his shirt away, aware of it landing on the floorboard with a thump.

Desire roared through her at the sight of him, lean yet muscled through the arms, chest and stomach. Well-earned signs of his hard work—a cowboy through and through, if she said so herself.

Reverently, she touched his chest. Sparse, coarse hair. Skin misted with summer dampness.

At her caress, his gaze went soft. Leaning down, he brushed a kiss over her lips.

"I can't seem to help myself with you," he whispered.

And neither could she. Felicia didn't usually spend her affection unwisely, without discretion. But now, it felt right, knowing he would be inside her soon.

Where he belonged.

Hesitantly, she latched her fingers into the rim of his jeans, running her knuckles over his belly, making him groan.

"Now," she said. "I want you now."

Her body applauded the command, thundering in ovation.

As he slipped one arm under her head to make her more comfortable in the cramped space, he nudged her with his erection, sliding against her. She was so ready for him.

"Not yet," he said. "Now that we're here, I aim to take my time with you."

She smiled, quietly jubilant, their pulses beating in counter tempo against each other's bodies.

When he palmed a breast, she couldn't help arching against him, closing her eyes and pressing her face against an arm she'd lifted over her head.

At this moment, with his thumb gliding circles around her nipple and bringing it to a sensitive peak, she was complete. Utterly feminine and full of life, able to give as much back to the world as it had given to her.

He bent his head, licked her nipple through the thin cotton of her blouse and silk of her bra, tracing the nub of it with his tongue while using his other fingers to shape her other breast. With expert care, he kneaded it, causing her to shift restlessly beneath him.

She could feel the wetness of his mouth even through the material, could feel him sucking and taking her gently between his teeth and pulling, just enough to send her into a searing frenzy.

As he unbuttoned her blouse, she wrapped her legs around him, wiggling ever so slightly, encouraging him.

He made a strangled sound then coaxed a hand inside her top, dipping his fingers into the cup of her bra and massaging until she thought she was going to churn into butter.

"You're so damned perfect," he murmured into her ear.

Every one of her nerve endings was on fire, prickling her skin with a light sheen of sweat. She wanted to thank him for how he was making her feel—like the woman she'd always known she could be—but the words caught in her throat.

He tugged down her bra until one breast was bared to him. With exquisite, maddening ease, he peeled open the other side of her top. Then her bra.

All his, every inch of her.

He pulled back a little, enough to lavish her with his gaze. Slowly, he settled his hands on her waist then floated them up, up, one thumb dipping into her belly button and making her buck. Both thumbs dragging up the center of her stomach while his fingers combed her ribs, tickling her. Palms claiming her stimulated breasts once again, as if he couldn't get enough of them.

Then, he traveled back down, the same worshipful gleam in his dark eyes—a look that stole her heartbeat clean away.

He mapped her hips, thumbs roaming her belly, sending more life into her with every lethargic motion. Oh….

Waves were rolling over her, starting between her thighs and washing upward, downward…all over. Warmth, a moon's reflection caught in the ripples of a tide, cleansing her.

He went lower still.

As he pushed up her skirt, the night air bathed her bare thighs. Then he spread her legs and ran his fingers down the inner flesh of them.

Felicia wanted to scream, wanted to cry with all the loveliness of this straining expectation. But instead, she exhaled on a shaking sigh as he traced the most tender part of her.

"Jack." She reached down, trying to take off her underwear, but she fumbled in her attempts.

"Here."

The silk breezed against her as he worked them off. Suddenly she felt vulnerable, open and unguarded. Excited by the air smoothing over places that were usually left private.

He'd left the underwear above her knees and was now divesting her of those flat shoes. Then he kissed his way from her ankle to the undies, maneuvering her legs and yanking the silk downward so that it was eventually gone, too.

"An expert?" she asked breathlessly.

With modesty, he shrugged, then slowly parted her legs again.

She gasped, her skin flaming in what was surely a body-encompassing blush while her skirt fell around her hips.

Almost casually, he bent one of her legs so he could wrap an arm around it, leaning against it. "You might remember my telling you that I've got a real liking for sweets."

He sketched a thumb between the wet folds of her, and Felicia winced, her hips imitating every stroke.

"Pies," he said, "ice cream…you."

He found a spot that made her even crazier, pressing against it, massaging until she dug her fingernails into her own thighs.

Repositioning himself, he moved down, cheek scratching against her leg. Felicia was beside herself with anticipation of what was to come.

Then it happened. The crush of his mouth against her, the pressure of his tongue licking, driving her to insanity. She rocked against him, making catlike sounds she didn't even know she was capable of.

A flood built against the walls of her body, trying to find release, crashing and breaking over and over again, dragging her out into an expanse of endless nothing only to push her under, where she couldn't get any air.

Jack must have noticed because he shucked off his jeans then slid on a condom. She panted, reached for him. Finally, he came back, his length prodding her as he braced himself on both arms, looking down on her.

"Felicia?"

She realized what he was asking. Even in her daze, she knew the ramifications of what they were about to do.

But she loved him more than she had thought it possible to love anyone, wanted him to be happy, wanted him to love her right back.

At any sacrifice.

"Jack."

The tone of her voice invited him in.

With a moan, he eased inside, so lovingly, so gently, she wondered if he really did feel more than he would admit for her.

She bit her lip, waited for the discomfort, the screeching of her body for it to stop.

There was a momentary tightness, leading only to fulfillment, the ever smoother feel of the man she loved stretching her body to fit him.

All thought was swept away with his first thrust. She echoed him, their rhythm starting out at a low flame, then flaring, speeding into an inferno that licked at her, sizzling and taking her over until she cried out from the burn of it.

As sweat dripped from his body to hers, their skin rubbing together in slick time, it felt as if steam were taking her over, hissing through her veins as fire turned to water, as she was tossed and turned and scorched from the inside out.

Then…then…

An explosion. A roar of heat so lethal that she didn't know if she existed anymore.

She cried out, consumed.

Melted into simmering water.

As Jack worked to his own climax, she held on, watched him as he clutched in what seemed like blissful agony, then spilled himself into the condom.

"Jack," she whispered, never wanting to let him go.

And she didn't—at least not for the beautiful afterglow, where he held on, too.

Returning all her affection and hope.

Telling her that they'd always be together.

Days later, after many nights spent in Felicia's arms, Jackson found himself knocked for a loop.

Half of him wondered what the hell he'd done in the pickup that night, giving in to his raging libido when he should have been listening to his conscience instead.

But the other half of him—the lower half, he would wager—was real damned glad he'd made love with Felicia.

Yet where did this leave him? Wanting more, that was what, even though he didn't have the faintest idea these days of just how much to give.

Not that he had a lot worth parceling out. He'd been straight with her about his decision never to have another family. And, although he wasn't sure she *truly* believed that he wasn't her last cowboy, he was relieved that he wasn't expected to be the baby maker/family man anymore.

At least, that was what he kept repeating to himself over and over again.

Now, as he sat in an old gazebo on Oakvale

property, he couldn't help sneaking glances at Felicia every few seconds.

Hair flowing freely down her back, a home-made crocheted red shawl covering her bared shoulders, a pink sundress making her look demure and flushed.

Damn, she was so…so…*Felicia.* One of a kind. Beautiful without even seeming to know it. Kind-hearted and open.

Much too good for him.

But, still… God, he needed her.

They were sitting around a table with Rip, Carlota, Emmylou and Deston Rhodes after having been invited to dinner while Bobby played with Joel and Noel—the twins from hell—again. Right now, the boys were with the twins' mother, bless her soul.

In the meantime, Felicia had translated all of Emmylou's damned good dishes into layman's terms for Jackson: beef Bourguignon, fava-bean paste over pasta, an eggplant dish, salad and fresh-baked bread, plus a selection of handmade chocolates for dessert.

As a bonus, they were also being treated to a quaint view of Oakvale—something most people never got to see. In the near distance, across a meadow, abandoned dude cabins stood as a reminder of a business the Rhodes family had turned their backs on decades ago. As Emmylou served coffee—strong and dark for

Jackson—he imagined city folk riding around, falling off their horses, dressing in Western costumes and pretending to go on cattle drives.

Emmylou poured the last cup for her husband, Deston, the wealthy CEO of his family's corporation, a man women would no doubt fall all over themselves for. Brown spiky hair with green eyes, a build that hearkened back to his days of playing quarterback for the Longhorns. Jackson couldn't help thinking that Felicia should have been with someone like Deston: successful, handsome, able to give her anything she wanted.

At the moment, Rip and Deston were chatting about beef prices while everyone else listened in. Even though Jackson could detect an undercurrent of anxiety in the old rancher's lackadaisical attitude, he couldn't get involved in the conversation. Not with Felicia putting a casual hand on his thigh.

Not with her working him up with just a single touch.

He must have wandered off into a sexual la-la land, because before he knew it, there was silence at the table.

Everyone was staring at him as if he should be answering some question.

Felicia squeezed his leg, holding back a smile at the same time.

"Sorry," he said, trying to put the sweet smell of

her hair and the soft feel of her body out of his mind. "I was off in the clouds without a wagon to ride in."

"I'm only noting to Deston," Rip said, a twinkle in his eyes, "that you'll be in charge of getting a good haul for them beeves this year. If you can keep your mind on it."

It was let's-poke-fun-at-Jackson hour. Every time he worked with the old man anymore, he never heard the end of how joyful Rip was to see a crank like Jackson finally come around to noticing Felicia's charms.

Dammit. It was too hard to hide what was going on between them, and Rip was no dummy anyway. That made having a personal life on the Hanging R next to impossible.

"My mind's where it needs to be," Jackson said, wondering if the same could be stated about his Johnson.

"At any rate," Carlota said, brown eyes showing her amusement, "I think you all make a cute couple."

Jackson slipped down in his chair. She hadn't just said that.

"Carlota." It was Emmylou. His savior? "Can't you see he's embarrassed? It's not nice to make fun of a man in love."

Nope, not a savior. And…er…love?

Jackson wanted to say something—*anything*—but Felicia came to his rescue. "Stop, you all." To the women, she said, "You promised to stay off the subject, thank you."

Emmylou grinned. "You're right. No need to shout out the truth when it's as big as day anyway."

Another inch lower in his chair.

Why was it that he couldn't find a word to say in his defense?

"Now, now." Rip held out his hands, looking for all the world like a judge on high in a cowboy hat and whiskers. "Jackson here shouldn't get all ruddy-faced about this. Right, Romeo? After all, he made a hell of a choice in our girl Felicia. In fact, I can already hear wedding bells clanging...."

Everyone laughed and shot Jackson fond looks—especially Felicia, who seemed so damned giddy that he almost didn't mind suffering for her smile.

Almost.

However, Deston finally took pity on Jackson, who was about ready to kick a hole through the gazebo floor and dig his way back to a place where cupid didn't come in the guise of an old-man busybody with a matchmaking complex.

"So..." Deston's voice boomed over everyone's hilarity. Attention captured, he leaned back in his chair, nodding at Jackson in a show of male unity. "How about those Astros?"

Mightily relieved, Jackson was the first to chime in with his opinion about the baseball team, having garnered information from Bobby during numerous discussions about the boys of summer. Jackson hadn't given a second thought to bats and balls for years and getting back into the former habit—the comfort of statistics and wins—soothed him, somewhat.

Thank goodness this particular conversation had swayed away from Jackson and Felicia and taken a safer course. One in which he had better footing.

Barely.

But near the end of it, when Felicia nestled her hand into his, Jackson went to mush all the same.

Yup, a touch was all it took.

He chanced a peek at her and their gazes locked, sending a rush of white-hot light through him.

He grinned back at her, feeling the flames, the rumble of longing and awareness.

But when he smelled the smoke, it only took him a moment to realize that the fire was all too real.

Chapter Twelve

Out in the old dude cabins, Bobby had been watching Joel and Noel do something he knew was wrong.

After telling their mom they were just going to hang around outside on the lawns, Joel and Noel had actually brought Bobby to the biggest cabin, a place where they weren't allowed to play. The one where a ladder let them climb to a high room and dangle their feet over the ledge so they could look down at all those dusty chairs and a spider-webbed bed.

Joel and Noel's mom had allowed them to wander around only if they stayed out of trouble, she'd said, but Bobby knew that wasn't what was happening right now.

Bobby glanced away from Joel, trying to pretend his friend wasn't doing what he was doing. He tried to take his mind off the trouble they could get into, tried to think of a way to be Joel and Noel's pal and still make Uncle Rip proud of him. His great-uncle trusted Bobby, and Bobby liked that. It made him feel like a grown-up. Besides, Uncle Rip had promised that Mrs. Krauss would give him a treat if he was good.

In his efforts to think of something to get out of the mischief he would no doubt get into, Bobby peered around the cabin.

Everything smelled weird here, like his parents' basement. The one they *used* to have.

Bobby swallowed and tried to be a tough guy, just like Jackson said he was. He thought about Mom and Dad all the time but didn't like to show how sad it made him. Crying was for babies.

"Watch this," Joel said.

Without thinking, Bobby looked.

Joel was holding a match right in front of his face and Noel was shrinking back from his brother.

"Mom's gonna kill you," Noel said.

"She's not gonna know." Joel was eight, so he could probably get away with a lot. "Not unless you tell her, tattletale."

"I'm not a tattletale."

"Then shut up."

Bobby didn't think a match was a good idea. Once, when he'd found a lot of them in the guest bathroom and lit one, his dad had spanked him. Bobby never got spanked, except for that time.

Still, he didn't know how to tell Joel to stop it. Especially now that his friend was sticking his finger in and out of the fire.

"Ouch!" Joel breathed in through his teeth and dropped the match.

Bobby leaned over the ledge, watching the flame flutter to the wooden floor. It floated to somewhere below where they were sitting, right in back of the ladder, so Bobby lost track of it.

Joel and Noel were watching, too, laughing.

"She-et," said Noel, who'd learned to say those kinds of things from the estate's gardeners.

Fear started to niggle at Bobby's stomach, stirring it up. It got like that when he knew there would be heck to pay, like the time he'd pinched Jo Ann Green near the eye after she'd kissed him. It'd left a big, red mark.

The boys watched the floor for a moment, but nothing happened. All that stayed behind was the smell of smoke from the match.

Bored now, Joel stood, hopped onto the upstairs bed then started jumping up and down on it.

"Come on," he said. "I ain't got any more matches! Mom used the rest of them on her ciggies."

Bobby finally spoke up, even though he felt stupid about it. Uncle Rip wouldn't want him hanging around Joel and Noel if he knew they were the type of kids who stole matches from their mom's purse.

"Let's go," Bobby said, standing. "I want to play outside."

While the twins stared at him, he thought he smelled smoke. Real smoke.

Bobby's gut squirmed even more.

"Ah." Joel continued to bounce. "Don't listen to the baby."

"Baby Bobby," Noel said, following his brother's lead and climbing onto the bed.

Giggling together, they jumped and jumped.

Bobby stood there, wondering what to do. He wasn't a baby. He was a tough guy, and he wasn't about to let Joel or Noel prove differently.

Still, tough guys could be smart, so Bobby sucked up all his courage and headed toward the ladder so he could go to his uncle Rip.

"Baby!" both the twins yelled.

But Bobby barely noticed because the flames were already licking their way up the ladder.

All he could do now was scream.

* * *

While Emmylou called 9-1-1 on a cell phone, everyone ran to the cabins.

Jackson got there first, but he was so distraught he could barely see the wooden dwellings, the smoke pouring out of one of them in particular.

And when he thought he heard the shouting—little voices crying for help—he almost stopped functioning altogether. The only thing that seemed to work in his body was his heart, which was thudding so rapidly that Jackson thought it was about to jump out of his throat.

Leroy. Lucas.

The flames of a never-ending nightmare.

Felicia and Deston skidded to a halt beside him. They had carried a cooler here, after emptying it of drinks and keeping the ice, a lot of which was melted.

Emmylou was making another rushed call, this one to Joel and Noel's mother.

"God, please let the boys be with her," Felicia said.

An emphatic shake of Emmylou's head almost slammed Jackson to the ground.

Bobby. He hadn't been imagining voices at all.

Without another thought, Jackson took hold of the shawl Felicia was wearing, tugged it off her shoulders and dipped it in the ice water.

"What're you doing?" she asked, frantic.

What I failed to do all those years ago with my sons.

God, he only hoped he could do some good this time, hoped he wouldn't be responsible for more lost lives.

"You know CPR," he said, remembering her stories about Oakvale from the Hanging R campfires.

"Yes."

"Then you, Emmylou and Carlota need to stay out here." He doffed his hat and threw it to the ground. "Those kids are in there and they'll need help when we come out."

"But—"

"Stay here, Felicia."

When he looked at her, it seemed to last an hour, although he knew he could only afford a second. He tried to tell her everything he was too damned stubborn to say, tried to apologize for not being the man she needed, even though he was doing his best.

But he couldn't wait any longer. Couldn't pour out his heart to her when he should have done it long before now.

With a final glance—one he hoped would convey everything—he whipped around, raising the dripping shawl to his face.

The fire was roaring by now, a low rumbling invitation for Jackson to come and get it.

To make up for what had happened to Leroy and Lucas, his two little babies.

His biggest regrets.

As he sprinted toward his own special hell, he thought he heard Felicia call out from behind him, her voice hoarse and terrified.

"I love you!"

Her words, imagined or not, almost tripped him up, but he couldn't turn around, couldn't go back to her like he wanted to and fall at her feet to say he was sorry.

Sorry for not opening up his heart.

And what exactly is in your heart? he thought. Just how do you feel about her, Jackson?

Adrenaline scrambled his body, his brain, making it almost impossible to think, to sort through questions that would have to wait.

As he approached, smoke surrounded him, embraced him with the acrid sharpness of the past. It closed him off from the world he was running from, stung his eyes and made time drag by in slow motion.

His worst enemy was back to claim him.

Nearby, Deston had shrugged out of his own shirt and dampened it. In silent agreement, both he and Jackson jogged up the cabin's stairs—

—until someone grabbed the shawl away from Jackson.

"What the…"

Rip McCain didn't stop to apologize, but merely put the material over his own face, blocking the smoke from entering his lungs, darting on ahead of Jackson into the wall of hazy, seething gray.

"Goddammit!" Jackson made a grab for the old man, but he was too late. "Get back here, Rip!"

He knew the rancher loved his nephew, but he wasn't using his head. He wasn't in any shape to be risking his life.

Not like Jackson, who would give his soul to fight fire with everything he had.

In the next instant, while Deston followed Rip inside, Jackson tore off his own shirt, sprinted back to the cooler to wet it, then zoomed back to where Rip had disappeared.

At the threshold.

It all came back to him in a flashing second: walls of heat keeping him from his babies. Wails that were drowned out by the rumble of destruction. A choking needle prick in his chest as the smoke sewed him up in a midnight shroud.

Dammit, it wasn't going to beat him this time.

He charged inside, the world going from the peace of a mild Texas sunset to a raging, crackling lower level of nightmare. Pressing the shirt to his face, he weaved around fallen, flame-speared furniture, a slanted piece of timber that had fallen.

Then he saw it.

Felicia's shawl pooled on the floor in a heap of crimson.

Rip? Where was he?

Cries of desperation caught his attention and Jackson glanced up to the loft. Three boys looked down at him, their T-shirts pulled up to cover their mouths, the whites of their huge eyes visible against the grime of their faces.

Bobby, Joel, Noel.

Sweet Jesus, they were still alive. A sob wrenched through Jackson but he conquered it, fueled with new energy.

Just you try to beat me up again, he said to the flames. *Just you try to take these boys from me.*

Deston was attempting to climb up to the loft, but the area was catching fire, leaving him without anything to hold onto. No success there.

Taking a different approach, Jackson stood beneath the kids, tying the shirt around his face bandanna style and opening his arms. He signaled for one of them to jump down.

Even though the loft was raised, it wasn't so high that Jackson couldn't handle a little flying body. He could save them, break their falls, even if it involved playing Superman.

Joel and Noel were sobbing, shaking their heads, but at Jackson's gesture, Bobby stood, his fists clenched at his sides.

Come on, Jackson thought. Please, dammit, jump.

And Bobby, the toughest of the tough, did.

The impact sent the air whooshing out of Jackson as he caught him, and he stumbled backward, clamping Bobby to him.

Safe. Finally.

Saved.

Just like one of his own, come back to life.

But he knew he didn't have this luxury. Clasping Bobby, who was shuddering with coughs, Jackson shuttled him outside where Felicia was waiting like an angel with welcoming arms, too. In the back of Jackson's mind, he heard sirens.

He had just enough time to run a hand over his son's hair…no, *Bobby's* hair…to assure himself that the coughing child was really okay.

When he smiled up at Jackson, it was almost enough to bring a man crashing to the ground in thankfulness.

And in…something Jackson didn't know how to describe.

Oh, God, thank God.

"Hang in there, Bob," he said, voice thick with emotion and smoke.

Then, readjusting his makeshift mask, Jackson ran back inside to find Deston, who handed off either a bawling Joel or Noel to him. The other man pointed toward a corner of the room and Jackson knew what he was saying.

Rip.

Jackson made quick work out of getting the twin into Carlota's waiting arms while Deston took care of the other child still inside the burning cabin.

Then Jackson made his final trip into the disaster, passing Deston and the other twin on their way out.

By now debris was flaring down from overhead, chunks of flame burning toward the floor like tiny falling meteors. Jackson scooped up Felicia's shawl—he wasn't sure why—and searched for the old rancher.

He found Rip pinned under a slab of timber, his leg mangled and caught.

Jackson yelled, angry at the world. A bolt of horror surged through him as he pushed at the sizzling wood. The momentary singe of fire on skin made him curse at the top of his lungs, but Jackson ignored the blinding pain.

Rip. Dammit, this was Rip, the man who'd taken Jackson in like a son. A good man with an unshakable moral code and a heart as big as the sky.

Straining, Jackson pushed at the timber. It finally gave way. As Rip moaned, Jackson slung him over his shoulders then sped toward the exit, bobbing around all the obstacles fate had put in his way.

When he got outside, he was greeted by the fire truck. Uniformed men and women were hopping off the vehicles, preparing to douse the cabin. Felicia, Emmylou and Carlota were grudgingly sacrificing their nursing duties to a couple of professional medical workers.

"Over here!" Jackson yelled.

Grunting with the effort, he carried Rip as far as he could from the wreckage, his back aching—but not as painfully as his soul.

As gently as possible, he lay Rip on the ground, Felicia's shawl covering his chest like spilled blood.

The old man's face was charred on one side, his right leg bent like a piece of steel caught in a car accident. The breath rasped in and out of him while he weakly clutched at Jackson's shoulder.

"Bob...."

"He's alive, Rip. Don't talk right now." Jackson couldn't help it. Years of damming back his anguish had finally battered him senseless, sucking all the tears right out of him. But now, they were threatening, seeping out of the corners of his eyes and down his cheeks in exhaustion and pure fear for this man he'd come to respect and love.

"You're going to be okay," Jackson choked out. Coughing, he tried to tell himself that it was the smoke that had gotten to his eyes, his throat.

Rip was moving his head back and forth. *No,* he seemed to be saying. *I'm not all right.*

"Sit still." Jackson tried to calm the stubborn old man, but he was shaking so hard he couldn't do much good.

Don't you leave us, Rip, he thought. Goddammit, don't you dare.

He couldn't even glance up to see what was keeping the medical staff, but he suspected that they were still tending to the boys.

Rip squeezed Jackson's shoulder again before a cough racked through him. His hand collapsed to the ground.

"Bobby," he managed to utter. "You."

One lone sob tore out of Jackson. He *knew* what Rip was trying to say. What he was asking him to do.

What made Rip think that Jackson could handle taking Bobby under his wing?

But if there was one thing he realized, it was that you didn't withhold promises from a man who thought he was going to die. Rip would be okay just as soon as a paramedic or EMT got over here. They would put an oxygen mask on him and everything would be back to normal.

Right, God? Jackson thought. *I don't talk to you much, not since Leroy and Lucas left me for you, but can't you wind the clock back to this afternoon so we can erase all this?*

A tiny weeping noise caught Jackson's attention, and he glanced up to see Felicia, tears streaming down her face as she dropped to her knees beside Rip. As she prepared to administer CPR,

Rip smiled at her, said something that sounded like "Markow... You... Bob...?"

And stopped breathing.

"No." Felicia braced her hands on his chest, started to pump, then switched to breathing into his mouth.

Jackson sat back on his heels, too stunned to move. His hands started to crackle with agony and his throat burned so badly that he thought he'd caught fire inside, that it would destroy him right along with everything else he loved.

Because that was how it went. His kids, Rip...

Caring was killing him. And everyone around him.

Felicia was back to working on Rip's chest. "Wake...up..."

When Jackson took his pulse, there was nothing, only Felicia's useless exertions.

Tenderly, Jackson put his arms around her, stopping her from doing any more. She collapsed against him, sobbing, her hand still on Rip as if she could bring the life back into him.

As she mourned, Jackson played the strong pillar, comforting her, keeping her upright.

Because his walls had gone back up today and he'd accepted what fate obviously intended for him to be.

The unfeeling rock everyone could lean on.

One that would eventually roll away when the burden became too much.

Chapter Thirteen

Rip's funeral was well attended, with flowers blanketing the Hanging R's living area. Although Felicia had volunteered to help, Jack had insisted upon making the arrangements, seeing to it that rented folding chairs were set up in front of the porch, where people could speak to the crowd about Rip. An urn that housed his ashes lingered on a gingham-clothed table. A group of his best friends would spread what was left of his body over the ranch later, returning Rip to the land he loved so much.

Now, as the windmill creaked a lonely song in the

faint wind, the attendees mingled with each other—
all 153 of them. Their murmurs comforted Felicia
only slightly. She was glad to see that so many people
in this county had loved Rip, but she was crushed by
the thought of never seeing him again.

She could count on her hands the number of times
she'd felt this torn apart. Her mother's, then her
father's death, the news from the doctor about her
chances to be a mom.

Her gaze snagged on Jack, who was standing
apart from all the others with Bobby at his side.
Both of them were wearing ranch clothing because
Jack believed that was what Rip would have wanted;
no fancy duds had ever graced the old man's frame,
so why should they dishonor him by starting such a
tradition now?

Bobby was leaning against Jack's leg, hugging it.
Jack himself rested one of his bandaged hands on
Bobby's curly head.

The picture jerked at Felicia's heartstrings. Two
lost souls who'd found each other.

And she wasn't anywhere near them, even though
her heart cried out to be.

One of her cousins kissed her on the cheek, trying
to make her feel better, and even though Felicia was
thankful, it would take more than kisses to make the
agony go away.

She thanked her cousin, then wandered over to

Jack, drawn to him, needing to be around him because he, more than anyone else, had adored Rip so much.

"How're you doing?" she asked, addressing Jack but bending down to Bobby so she could hold his hand. From the way Jack had been looking at her these past days, she wondered if he remembered that he'd even made love to her. It didn't seem so now, with his eyes gone dark and still, like black pools devoid of life.

Rip's death had cast too much of a pall on their daily lives for anything else to be a priority, she supposed. Instead, Felicia had given Jack his space, needing to feel his arms around her yet knowing time could heal him just as well as she could.

At least, that was what the negative voices in her head were saying.

"I'm doing fine." He was watching her, almost as if he was regretting something. "How're you holding up?"

"Fine."

See, even their conversations had been reduced to exercises in futility.

And she knew exactly why.

Leroy and Lucas, now Rip. Figurative blood on the hands of a man who thought he was the one responsible for putting it there.

Felicia caught sight of Mrs. Krauss standing on the porch steps with a plate of cookies in hand.

Searching the crowd for Bobby, no doubt. Since Rip had died, the older woman had rarely come out of her room, Jack had told Felicia. Sure, she still cooked and cleaned, but she didn't socialize with anyone except for Bobby, who received lots of extra loving from the hausfrau.

Clearly, her heart was as broken as the rest of theirs.

"Someone's got a treat for you," Felicia said to Bobby as Mrs. Krauss spotted him and urgently waved him over.

"I'm not real hungry," he said.

"I know."

Bobby was back to being the serious boy he'd arrived as. It made Felicia want to cry, but instead, she embraced him.

He returned her affection, clinging to her.

"It's okay," she whispered. "I miss him so much it hurts, too."

He drew away, eyes moist, though he didn't give in to tears. Bobby tended to mourn alone in his own room, where Felicia had stumbled upon his grief a few times.

"My mom used to say hugs are like big Band-Aids on an owie," he said.

Smiling, Felicia gave him a pat on the back as he began walking toward Mrs. Krauss, his shoulders stiff, a little boy with big-man responsibilities. A kid who'd lost his parents and a wonderful uncle in the space of a month.

It wasn't fair, Felicia thought. But then again, what was?

When Bobby got to the older woman, she took him into her arms in a bear hug and Bobby sank right against her as if she were a comfy pillow.

Felicia waited a beat then glanced up to find Jack watching her with unguarded longing in his eyes. The intensity of it rattled her.

But then he looked away.

Legs quivering, she managed to stand anyway. She hated this disconnection and wanted to offer respect by not pushing herself on him, yet it felt as if she were losing ground.

Losing him.

Hadn't he heard her say *I love you?*

Didn't he care?

There was only so much longer she could take this, but Bobby still came first. Best to address that situation before anything else.

"Have you decided what you're going to do?" she asked.

"About Bobby?"

He knew damned well what she was talking about. She'd been there when Rip had all but asked Jack to take care of him. Had been there when Rip had seemed to ask her, too....

But maybe that was wishful thinking. One thing was for certain, though—Jack had recently been informed that Rip had made legal preparations for him to take guardianship of Bobby in case of an emergency. Now it was up to the courts.

And to Jack.

"You know I can't be Bobby's substitute parent," he said.

Frustration took her over. "He needs someone, and Rip died thinking that it would be you."

"I didn't know what else to do when he was lying there…." A muscle ticked in his cheek as he tightened his jaw. "I want to…"

His voice skidded to a stop, and Felicia caught her breath.

"Go on," she said softly.

His gaze followed Bobby, who was taking a seat in the front row next to Mrs. Krauss. But before Felicia could rejoice, Jack's shoulders slumped.

"You know me well enough by now, Felicia. I'm not the best option for him."

He didn't have to say the rest. The look in his eyes filled in the blanks.

And I'm not the best option for you, either.

She was speechless, thrashed to a wordless heap.

All she could do was watch Dutch, Carter and Stoverson herding the funeral attendees into their chairs.

There it was.

Like all of her ex-boyfriends, Jack had failed to fall for her. And why not? No matter how hard she tried to keep hold of their affection, it never worked out.

But this time it mattered much more than usual.

Good God, he was perfect for her—couldn't he see that? She hadn't even hurt during their lovemaking as she'd feared. Whether that was due to a grand design or the medication she'd been taking, it didn't matter. Jack was the one. Why couldn't he admit it?

"And here I thought you might have a feeling or two for me," she said.

"I do. But all along I told you not to get your hopes up."

Anger was starting to eat at her, but it wasn't directed toward Jack. Not all of it, anyway, because he had warned her time and again and, fool that she was, she hadn't listened. No, her disgust was more toward life itself, circumstances, *fate.*

"So that means you're through with Bobby, too?" she asked. Funny, she didn't sound as ticked off as she sounded wounded.

Jack paused then fixed that haunted gaze on her again.

"Have you asked yourself how effective I'd be raising a child? Think about this. My sons died in my care. Rip expired in my arms. What's going to happen to Bobby?"

Enough was enough. "So that's it. You're cursed, huh, Jack? You don't believe you can care for another person…*ever.* Why can't you believe that you deserve a second chance? I mean, look what you did with Bobby already. You saved his life. Doesn't that make up for anything?"

For a fleeting moment, something close to hope lit up his face, but it was gone like smoke in a breeze.

"Rip asked you to take Bobby," she said, resting her hand on his arm. "He trusted you. Admired you. He saw how much Bobby adores you."

When Jack spoke, his voice sounded like barbed wire, tangled and sharp. "I'm not the one to take on such a job. I'll hang around until someone more suitable can be found for Bobby, but then…"

Her dreams dropped to her feet, shattering. "You're going to leave?"

He opened his mouth to answer, then shut it, re-capturing whatever words he was about to offer. At the same time, Stoverson stepped up to the micro-phone on the porch and started the ceremony. Next to him, Rip's ashes waited in the urn, patient as always.

As the crowd laughed softly at anecdotes about the old rancher—and there were many—Felicia drew further into herself. It was almost as if Jack had turned into a ghost beside her, a memory of what her future might have been.

So this was it. He would go his way, she would go hers. Fun times while they'd had them, yes? Obviously, Felicia's big mistake had been in making Carlota's prediction what she wanted it to be, molding the words into something that wasn't meant to have ever produced results.

But her love had been real, she thought, tears starting to heat up her eyes, to blur those rose-colored glasses she insisted on wearing.

In fact, she wouldn't regret loving Jack for anything, even if he couldn't do the same for her.

Yet by God, he couldn't even bring himself to love Bobby, and didn't they both deserve more?

From his spot on the porch, Stoverson, the preppiest, most Ivy League cowboy she'd ever seen, began to lose composure. His voice trembled as he talked.

"I'd never seen anyone quite like Rip McCain before I ended up here. Not that I'd ever even worked on a ranch anyway. But Rip didn't seem to mind. I gave him a résumé like you would for some kind of office job and he just laughed—you know, that laugh that came from deep within him, a wheeze that would shake him apart if he didn't stop it soon?"

Everyone chuckled, remembering Rip's eternal good nature.

"What he told me that day will stay with me forever." Stoverson looked up to the sky, as if channeling his boss. "'Son,' he said, 'a cowboy is born, not made. You've either got the goods or you don't. And, by golly, I feel you've got the cowboy way in you.'"

Silence weighed down the air, punctuated by sniffs. Felicia didn't bother to hold back her weeping, especially when Jack touched her shoulder with his bandaged hand then walked away.

She suspected he was just as stricken as any of them were, but damn him, he wouldn't give in to it.

Would *never* give in to it.

Maybe it was time for her to stop wishing he would.

She wandered away from the ceremonies, too, not knowing where to go, Stoverson's final words ringing in her ears.

"What I'll always remember about Rip," he said, "is that he was the real thing. The best of what this country was built on, a man who'd do anything for his neighbors and who ran on pride and hard work. Rip McCain was the last of them all right, because you'll never find that kind of fortitude again.

"Yes," he added, breaking down in his own tears, "that man was the last cowboy we'll ever see."

Stunned, Felicia stopped in her footsteps, the vibrations of Carlota's prediction chiming through her.

Rip. Last cowboy. Bobby?

Or was she just wishing for something that would never happen?

Then again…

She spotted the little boy in the front row, alone while he forlornly watched Stoverson stumble down from the porch, too young to be left alone without parents to guide him.

All Felicia wanted to do was start believing again.

An hour later, as the funeral wound down, Jackson was still collecting himself, hidden from sight near the back of the barn while emptying his mind and listening to all the people praise his beloved boss.

Rip McCain. The best there ever was. Never married, never had children. The Hanging R was the closest thing he'd had to progeny.

Damn, Jackson wished he were here.

He missed Rip's strange colloquialisms, his golden work ethic. Hell, Jackson even missed his penchant for sticking his nose where it didn't belong.

Imagine, he thought, how the old man even thought *I* could do a good job of bringing up Bobby.

As Jackson finally allowed thoughts of the boy to come back into him again, a surprising glow of emotion warmed him, spreading from his chest and up into his throat, where it burned and made it hard to catch any oxygen.

Rip would have been disappointed by Jackson's decision to leave Bobby to someone else. And he would have shaken that gray head at the way Jackson had denied Felicia's love just to make himself feel stronger.

A real man would never act as Jackson had. Not by Rip McCain's standards.

Standards that had seeped into Jackson's bones bit by bit, until he sometimes even felt as if Rip, like a stubborn skeleton, had been holding up Jackson's tired body for the last few days.

But Felicia had propped up Jackson, too, chasing away his self-doubt, making him think he could believe in himself again.

In all truth, before the fire, he'd even thought he could live up to all their expectations, with the way Felicia looked at him as if he were some sort of hero.

So what was his problem now?

Didn't he love Felicia? Couldn't he?

And Bobby…

Dammit, thinking about it lifted him up yet scared him at the same time because he knew that he didn't want to live without the little boy, either.

Earlier, when he'd told Felicia that he was planning on leaving the Hanging R to continue drifting, it had seemed to Jackson as if he'd brought a form of death to her, too—killing the hopes she'd so innocently pinned on him.

He felt sick to his stomach even thinking about it. Unlike the way he'd clung to the pain Leroy and Lucas's tragedy had brought him, he found no warped satisfaction in punishing himself for what

was happening with Felicia. It was in no way justi-
fied or poetic. He wouldn't make himself a better
man by turning his back on her and Bobby.

In fact, had he really improved all that much by
beating himself up over the death of his sons?

Deep in his gut, he knew the answer, knew
Felicia had been right every single time she'd told
him to move on.

To live again.

He closed his eyes, hearing the shuffles and
muted discussion of the funeral crowd breaking up.

To live like Rip wouldn't get the opportunity to.

Not long ago, Jackson had run head first into a
fire, dammit. Why didn't he have the courage to step
up to a good-hearted, loving woman and tell her how
he really felt, how afraid he was to raise another boy,
even if his heart already belonged to the little guy?

The image of Felicia cuddling Bobby as if he
were her own thrust into him once again. A natural
mother. A son in need of parents.

He knew what he had to do.

What he *wanted* to do, deep inside his soul.

Pushing away from the barn wall and forcing
himself to walk into the open, his pulse began thrum-
ming against his skin.

When he came around the other side of the barn,
he searched for her in a throng of mourners who
were saying their goodbyes to Rip's ashes.

But she was nowhere in sight.

Panic caught at him. Had he finally chased her away? Was it too late to make amends this time?

God, if he could find her, he wouldn't back down this time. God, God, God....

He continued seeking her, finding Dutch and Carter hovering near a stand of flowers, quietly surveying the crowd, their faces drawn and lined with sorrow. Mrs. Krauss stood with her hand on Rip's urn, as if touching it would suffice for the real thing. J-Wayne lay with his head in his paws, keeping her company, keeping his eye out for a master who was never coming back.

Jackson could almost hear the old man right now.

You go get little Markowski, right quick, son. Time's awastin'.

"I'm trying, Rip," Jackson whispered.

He searched inside the cabin for her. No success. But he did hear the soft creak of a gliding porch seat that Rip kept near the back door.

Fisting his hands, Jackson stepped outside, his life coming into still focus before him.

There on that faded wooden seat, Felicia held Bobby. The boy was sleeping, sweet features arranged in momentary peace as she rocked him back and forth, smoothing the curls back from his face. The wind fluttered her angel-gold hair as she gazed at the hills in the near distance.

It was as if the hand of time had struck midnight in Jackson, ringing every cell of his body until he came together in the chaos, becoming whole again.

He was finally home, wasn't he?

Overwhelming joy made it hard to swallow, hard to get a hold of himself. And even though he started to tremble, he was stronger than ever.

"You're still here," Jackson said, keeping his voice low, although it seemed to echo over the landscape with his relief.

Felicia sent him an oddly jubilant grin, resting a hand over Bobby's ear while pressing his head against her chest. His little feet in those teeny tennis shoes looked so helpless as his legs sprawled over the seat.

"What made you think I'd leave?" she asked.

Unruffled, as calm as a pond at sun break.

His Felicia, a woman who never seemed to stop believing that he would come around.

There was room next to her, but Jackson didn't presume to sit. Not yet. Instead, he walked down the stairs, hoping he wouldn't break the serenity of this picture.

This view of what his life was meant to be.

He bent, stroked a bandaged finger over Bobby's chubby cheek. "I was wrong about what I said back there. About moving on."

She lay her cheek on Bobby's head. Her smile only grew bigger.

A mother and child, he thought.

"Are you telling me you're staying, Jack?"

He bit down on his emotion for a moment, too consumed by it to control his reaction. But then, at the hopeful lift of her brows, he seemed to explode—a laugh, a sob, he wasn't sure what it was he was doing.

He only knew that it felt damned good.

"Hell, yeah, I'm staying for as long as you'll have me." He took a breath, cupped a wounded hand over her jaw. "I want to hear you laughing every morning. I want to hear all the stories about your millions of relatives. I want to show everyone how damned much I love you, Felicia."

She closed her eyes, let out a sigh at the same time. "I think I've been waiting forever to hear you say that."

Still standing, he laughed, took off his hat and brought his forehead to hers. "I suppose I have a way of keeping you in suspense, huh?"

"I'd say." She opened her eyes, rubbed her nose against his, nuzzling him. "Up until an hour ago I thought life had gone down the drain, but then I realized that I just needed to be patient for a touch longer."

Felicia. This limitless optimism was going to be a part of his life.

And Bobby's life.

Unable to trust his knees much longer, Jackson finally sat down, fastening his fingers into her hair, filling himself with her scent, her presence. His future.

Jeez, he was really going to do this. Was going to take a wife *and* a child.

"Did you hear Stoverson talking?" she asked, giving him a reprieve.

"I wasn't listening so closely." Jackson had been too deaf with grief.

"Well, something he said made everything click into place, just like Rip is sitting in a comfortable somewhere fitting a puzzle together." She beamed. "'The last cowboy will make you a mother.' It was about Rip the whole time, Jack. He wants to make us a family."

She paused, probably afraid he'd change his mind again with the return of the Prediction.

The fact that she was talking about Carlota's visions or about the rancher as if he were still here should have put fear into Jackson, but it didn't. It only stirred up some of the bitterness over Rip's death, at the scheme of things in general because life had seen fit to take such a man from them.

So she thought that Rip was the one who'd made her a mother? Through Jackson? Through their love for Bobby?

A flash of conscience whirled through Jackson's mind: him talking about Rip during that heartfelt cowboy speech he'd given to Felicia that day in Wycliffe.

Maybe there's one cowboy left, he'd said. He'd been referring to Rip, all right. A scrap from the canvas of the old west, a stalwart throwback.

A part of the Prediction.

But why had the powers that be decided Rip needed to die for Jackson's and Felicia's happiness? It made no sense.

Felicia must have sensed the frustration in him. "I can't explain life, either, but Rip trusted you. He knew that, if anything happened to him, you'd be the perfect dad for Bobby." She laughed sadly. "I guess he went a lot on instinct, like he did when he hired Stoverson."

"Or when he hired me. Rip didn't know much about where I came from or what I was about, but he handed over his accounting books like I was meant for them."

She rested her fingers on his arm. "And he made you Bobby's guardian."

That glow welled up in him again, like a fountain that had been fixed after rusting away for years and years. He wasn't used to having this hope trickle through him, washing away all those clinging doubts.

But it was so right.

Jackson turned to face Felicia and Bobby, too overcome to say anything. Running a gaze over the child—*his* child, from now on, God help him—he rejoiced in the way Bobby's lashes fanned over his pinkened cheeks, how his mouth pouted in sleep, how he rested without nightmare or worry in Felicia's embrace.

Jackson knew how it felt. He brushed his fingertips over her temple, down her cheekbone, memorizing the openhearted beauty of her face.

"I love you," he said again, almost as if to reassure himself that this was really happening. "And I want to start over. Make things right for you…and Bobby."

Her eyes were blue mirrors, reflecting his affection right back at him. "I love you, too, Jack."

His soul seemed to crack open, forcing out every dark moment he'd held to himself, every remnant of self-hatred he'd lived with for so long.

In their place he found the warmth of a healing balm, a nest for love to grow and flourish. A field basking under the sun of a new day.

He smiled at the calm of it and Felicia leaned forward, careful not to disturb Bobby. Jackson himself didn't need any persuasion to do the same.

Their lips met in a gentle pulse of contact, a promise more golden than rings or the sunshine itself. With every brush of their mouths, he felt his heart being given over to her, laid out for her taking.

When Bobby shifted in Felicia's arms, they reluctantly pulled away from each other, though Jackson still kept his hand nestled near her neck.

He wasn't about to let go.

"Jack?" asked the little boy, his voice fuzzy with sleep.

"Right here."

Bobby blinked and, with what might have been a grin, went right back to sleep, obviously too exhausted for anything more.

Felicia's heart expanded just by watching Bobby and Jack. A family, and she was in the middle of it now.

Where she'd always wanted to be.

He was watching her again: the rough-and-tumble features, the mouth that had just kissed her, the eyes that shouted out his love for her…

They were all hers—the way things were meant to be.

As Jack slipped his arm around her, Felicia sighed into him, hugging Bobby closer. Soon they would be riding into the country to spread Rip's ashes, to give him back to the land and to watch the grass grow over those same dusty patches next year.

Time and tide, she thought. Birth and death.

She glanced at Bobby again, knowing that he might be the only son she would ever have.

But that didn't matter, because Bobby would be enough son for her. He'd make her just as proud as a child of her own body would and, when it came right down to it, love was love.

And she had enough of it to last all their lifetimes.

Yes, she and Jack would see Bobby grow, just like the grass. They would be his parents, even if he hadn't come to them in the traditional way. They would raise him to remember his great-uncle, to appreciate the sacrifices Rip had made for all of them.

Jack tightened his hold around her and rested a hand on Bobby's leg. Cheerfully, Felicia leaned into him and watched the sun sink over the hills, the trees.

The grass that was already growing around them.

Epilogue

One year later

Jack laughed right along with the table of Markowski relatives who'd been invited over to the Hanging R to celebrate Bobby's birthday.

"Na zdrowie!" said Uncle John as he toasted the other adults with a glass of soda. "To your health!"

They all raised their drinks to each other and sipped. Aunt Grace stopped midway through and toasted another table; it was full of giggling children, balloons and used wrapping paper that Bobby had torn off his presents in glee. Felicia sat on a bench next to him, snapping pictures and generally keeping the peace.

"To Bobby," Aunt Grace said, "and his seven candles!"

Another round of soda guzzling followed and, as Aunt Jean continued the fun by suggesting a toast for the highballs they'd be drinking tonight after the kids went home, Jack took a break.

He leaned his elbows on the table and watched his wife and his adopted son, who was dressed like a cowboy with chaps and the whole nine yards, while he tore into another present.

Every time Bobby grew another inch, Jack felt his gratitude bloom, too. Much to everyone's surprise, the Hanging R was getting back on its feet with some creative bookkeeping from Jack—and a hefty loan from Deston that would be paid off within the next thirty years. They'd instituted an "old-time cattle drive" in the spring and fall to bring in more cash and Jack was making arrangements to breed horses, as well.

Even though Rip had entertained too much stubborn pride to take another person's money, Jack found no shame in it—as long as hard work would pay it off. He felt certain that Rip would have eventually come around and taken a loan to keep Bobby happy and healthy anyway.

So Jackson followed in the invisible footsteps of the man he aspired to be like, taking Rip's place the best he could, paying homage to him every day. After all, maybe there would come a time when Bobby could be a *real* cowboy, owning this spread and working it. Granted, the boy showed a lot more interest in academics than agriculture, but Jack hadn't let go of the dream.

Still, he realized that *he* just might be the last cowboy the Hanging R ever saw.

Uncle John nudged Jack with an elbow. He smelled of licorice and tobacco.

"You off in the ether?" the older man asked.

As Jack's gaze met Felicia's, he nodded. "Cloud nine."

Chuckling, Uncle John left him alone, probably knowing a lost cause when he saw one.

Across the table, Felicia and Jack grinned at each other like two starstruck kids. Marriage hadn't siphoned away their passion—it had built on it, day by day.

Even during Felicia's surgery and follow-up doctor visits, they'd remained happy, especially since the doctors were more optimistic about her chances of conceiving now.

Jack warmed, his heart expanding with the heat. He and Felicia were sure having some fun trying for a baby, and her continuing hope was an inspiration to him—a lesson in strength.

"Dad?" It was Bobby, calling for him.

Jack rose from his seat and came over to his son, touching his wife's shoulder as he looked down at Bobby. The child was holding up a large model T. rex with movable parts.

"Cool, huh?" Bobby said.

Jack nodded. Yeah, cool. Bobby still kept that wooden dinosaur Jack had carved for him but, slowly but surely, it had gotten buried under more toys in his closet.

His little boy, growing up. Ouch.

It was a nice hurt, though, the way life worked. A second chance to see how Leroy and Lucas would've turned out.

Now, as Bobby went back to his business and oohed and aahed over a present that reflected his new hobby—a chemistry set—a beaming Felicia kissed Jack's hand.

Now, his entire body exploded with joy, with all the love he'd been too afraid to feel before he'd met her.

She'd taught him that it was okay to wish, to persevere in the darkness of doubt and impossibility. And he had taken the lesson and used it for the benefit of his new family, putting his work and faith into resurrecting the Hanging R.

"Need a break?" Jackson asked his wife.

"Hey." She stood, kissed him, her lips warm against his. "I'll never need a break from you two."

Openly, lovingly, Jack wrapped his arms around

her. He loved her so much that words wouldn't suffice. Instead, he allowed his actions to speak for him—his every adoring gesture.

A smile washed over his mouth as he kissed his wife then watched Bobby have fun with his cousins and friends. In the background, his relatives were still toasting everything the world had to offer.

Once upon a time there'd been a prediction about a last cowboy, he thought, snuggling Felicia right next to him so she fit in every way.

And, in the end, after surviving Rip, maybe Jack really *was* the last cowboy on this ranch, one who had made Felicia a mother to Bobby—and maybe to another unborn child someday.

Maybe the prediction hadn't even come to fruition, he thought.

As she drew away and sent a saucy glance to him on her way to the cabin, Jack looked up at the sky and winked at Rip.

Who said he didn't believe in fate?

* * * * *

Look for Crystal Green's next thrilling book,
BAITED.

When Kat Espinoza agrees to grant
a dying friend's wish, she has no idea
what kind of danger awaits her....

Coming October 2006 to Silhouette Bombshell.

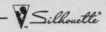

SPECIAL EDITION™

BABY BONDS

**A new miniseries by
Karen Rose Smith coming this May**

THE SERIES BEGINS WITH

CUSTODY FOR TWO

Shaye Bartholomew had always wanted a child,
and now she was guardian for her friend's
newborn. Then the infant's uncle showed up,
declaring Timmy belonged with him.

Could one adorable baby forge a
family bond between them?

*And don't miss
THE BABY TRAIL,
available in July.*

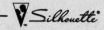

SPECIAL EDITION™

***Luke Tucker knew he
shouldn't get involved.***

"Mary J. Forbes is an author who really knows how
to tug on the heartstrings of her readers."
—*USA TODAY* bestselling author Susan Mallery

TWICE HER HUSBAND
by Mary J. Forbes

What he and Ginny Tucker Franklin had
shared was over, had been for ten years.
But when she returned to town, needing
his help, years fell away. All the loneliness of
the past decade vanished.

He wanted her as his wife again.

Available May 2006 wherever books are sold.

Silhouette®

BOMBSHELL™

ATHENA FORCE

CHOSEN FOR THEIR TALENTS.
TRAINED TO BE THE BEST.
EXPECTED TO CHANGE THE WORLD.

The women of Athena Academy are back.
Don't miss their compelling new adventures
as they reveal the truth about their founder's
unsolved murder—and provoke the wrath of a
cunning new enemy....

FLASHBACK
by Justine DAVIS

Available April 2006 at your favorite retail outlet.

MORE ATHENA ADVENTURES
COMING SOON:

Look-Alike by Meredith Fletcher, May 2006
Exclusive by Katherine Garbera, June 2006
Pawn by Carla Cassidy, July 2006
Comeback by Doranna Durgin, August 2006

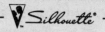

SPECIAL EDITION™

**Bound by fate, a shattered family renews
their ties—and finds a legacy of love.**

Family BUSINESS

HER BEST-KEPT SECRET

by Brenda Harlen

Jenny Anderson had always known
she was adopted. But a fling-turned-serious
with Hanson Media Group attorney
Richard Warren brought her closer than ever
to the truth about her past. In his arms,
would she finally find the love she's
always dreamed of?

Available in May 2006
wherever Silhouette books are sold.

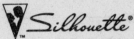